AN ANGEL IN HELL

Barbara Cartland, the celebrated romantic novelist, historian, playwright, lecturer, political speaker and television personality, has now written nearly two hundred books. She has had a number of historical books published and several biographical ones, including a biography of her brother, Major Ronald Cartland, who was the first Member of Parliament to be killed in the war. The book has a preface by Sir Winston Churchill.

In private life, Barbara Cartland is a Dame of Grace of St John of Jerusalem, and one of the first women, after a thousand years, to be admitted to the Chapter General. She has fought for better conditions and salaries for midwives and nurses, and, as President of the Hertfordshire Branch of the Royal College of Midwives, she has been invested with the first Badge of Office ever given in Great Britain, which was subscribed to by the midwives themselves. She has also championed the cause of old people and founded the first Romany Gypsy Camp in the world. It was christened 'Barbaraville' by the gypsies.

Barbara Cartland is deeply interested in Vitamin Therapy and is President of the National Association for Health.

D0715297

By the same author in Pan Books

For other titles by Barbara Cartland
please see page 172

BARBARA CARTLAND

AN ANGEL
IN HELL

A Pan Original

Pan Books London and Sydney

First published 1976 by Pan Books Ltd,
Cavaye Place, London SW10 9PG
© Barbara Cartland 1976
ISBN 0 330 24535 X

Printed and bound in Great Britain by
Hunt Barnard Printing Ltd, Aylesbury, Bucks.

Author's Note

The way in which Monte Carlo was described and denounced at the end of the last century is not exaggerated. It was considered by the clergy of almost every other nation 'a hell' on earth.

The newspaper articles are authentic.

To-day Point de Cabéel is known as Cap Estel and on it is the loveliest small hotel I know. The garden is exactly as I have described it and it has a flight of forty white marble steps from the terrace.

I have used the old spelling of Eza for Eze and St. Hospice is now Cap Ferrat.

Monte Carlo is still to me as beautiful, romantic and exciting as it has been ever since François Blanc opened the Casino in 1858.

Chapter One
1898

"I am sorry it happened so suddenly, Ancella," Sir Felix Johnson said in his quiet voice which had earned him the reputation of having the best bed-side manner in London.

"It is better that way," Lady Ancella Winn replied. "I would not have wanted Papa to go on enduring suffering and misery as he has these past years."

"He has been a very difficult patient," Sir Felix said, "and I can only commend you, Ancella, as being the most dutiful and exceptional daughter I have ever known in the whole of my long career."

"Thank you, Sir Felix," Ancella replied with a faint smile.

"I am worrying that perhaps your father's death has been a great shock," Sir Felix said kindly.

"No, not a shock," Ancella answered. "I was expecting it."

Sir Felix looked at her in a puzzled manner.

The Earl of Medwin had indeed been ill for a long time, but it was the sort of disease that usually prolonged itself almost indefinitely.

As if she knew that Sir Felix was waiting for an explanation Ancella, with the colour rising slightly in her cheeks, said:

"I sometimes know about . . . such things. I knew before Mama died that there was no . . . hope."

"You mean you were clairvoyant?"

"I suppose you might call it that. My Nurse, who was Scottish, used to describe it as being 'fey'. It is just that sometimes I feel an inexplicable conviction about things, and ever since I was a child it has always proved right."

"That is very interesting," Sir Felix said, "but what I would like you to tell me is whether you have a conviction about what you should do now."

Ancella made a little helpless gesture with her hands.

"That is something quite different," she said, "and quite frankly I have no idea."

"That is what worries me," Sir Felix said.

He had not only been Doctor to the Earl for over twenty years, but he was also a friend, and he was genuinely very fond of the Earl of Medwin's only child, Lady Ancella Winn.

He looked at her now with speculative eyes as she moved across the room to stand looking out of the window at the unkempt and untidy garden which looked desolate in the cheerless gloom of a January morning.

She was very fair and her skin, normally very white, was almost startlingly so after her father's sudden death.

"She is lovely!" Sir Felix told himself, and as Ancella turned her large grey eyes towards him he said:

"Ought you not to think about what you should do before your relations arrive and the heir to the title inevitably takes over?"

"Cousin Alfred, I understand, will not live here," Ancella answered. "He has always disliked the house and has no intention of spending any money on repairing it or keeping up the grounds. As you must know, Sir Felix, it would have been quite impossible for Papa, if he had not died, to hold on very much longer."

"I am aware of that," Sir Felix said, "and anyway there could be no question of your living here with your cousin."

"No, indeed," Ancella agreed quickly. "I have never liked Cousin Alfred and Papa positively disliked him!"

"So he has often told me," Sir Felix said. "Well then, what is the alternative?"

"Aunt Emily, or perhaps Aunt Edith," Ancella replied. "Oh, Sir Felix, I do not think I could bear it!"

Sir Felix could understand her feelings when he remembered the elderly grim-faced maiden ladies who had always disapproved of the independence Ancella had enjoyed after her mother's death.

Her father had let her do more or less as she wished, provided that she kept house for him and was there when he wanted her to listen to his grumbles about money and his constant harangues with his relatives.

When he became ill he had refused to have a Nurse – not that they could have afforded one – and had relied entirely on Ancella to look after him and be at his beck and call from first thing in the morning until last thing at night.

In fact she was also frequently wakened during the night; but she never complained, and Sir Felix had often asked himself what other girl of her age would have been so efficient or so willing to carry out his instructions.

Now, as he considered the Winn relations, he found himself thinking that none of them would make Ancella's life anything but a misery.

They were all very narrow, strait-laced, almost puritanical in their outlook, and the Earl had undoubtedly been right when he referred to them as 'a lot of old hypocritical, psalm-singing spinsters!'.

"If only I had some talents," Ancella said with a little sigh. "I can ride, I can sew, I can dance – when I get the chance! And I can speak several languages."

She gave a little laugh.

"None of that sounds to me to be saleable!"

"You can speak French?" Sir Felix asked.

"Like a Parisian – at least that was what the old *Mademoiselle* who taught me always said!" Ancella replied with a smile.

"That gives me an idea," Sir Felix said. "You may think

that it is an impertinence, you may laugh at me for suggesting it, but it might be a solution."

Ancella walked towards him to put her hand on his arm.

"You know, Sir Felix, that anything you suggested to me I should know was meant kindly and as a true friend. I have often wondered what we should have done without you these past months when Papa was so difficult and would refuse to do anything he was told."

She sighed before she went on:

"You were the only person he trusted, and I often thought we have imposed on your kindness and your friendship, when he continually asked you to come here when you were so busy in London."

Sir Felix put his hand over hers.

"Anything I have done, my dear, has been a pleasure, and I mean that!"

"And what is more," Ancella said quietly, "you have never sent us a bill!"

"Nor do I intend to do so," Sir Felix replied. "When I was a young man your father honoured me with his friendship. That meant a great deal to me in those days when I was unknown and struggling. So anything that I have done has been only a very small recompense for what I owe him."

For the first time tears came into Ancella's eyes.

"Thank you, Sir Felix!" she said. "I have always known how lucky I have been that you were there and I could rely on you."

"Then I am going to talk to you now both as a friend and as a Doctor," Sir Felix said, "so let us sit down, Ancella, and be comfortable while we do so."

She obeyed him, sitting upright in the chair, her hands in her lap like a child who is about to have a lesson.

Sir Felix seated himself opposite her on the other side of the fire-place.

In his long frock-coat and high, elegantly-tied cravat

which sported a large pearl pin, he was an impressive figure, as befitted the Physician in Ordinary to the Royal family who was tremendously in demand amongst the fashionable society which followed Queen Victoria's lead.

Ancella was aware that by coming down from London at a moment's notice when a groom had brought him the news that the Earl of Medwin was dead, he had probably created chaos amongst his wealthy patients who would be expecting him to call on them at this time of the day.

But she knew as she sent for him that Sir Felix would not fail her, and he had in fact arrived at Medwin Park near Windsor in almost record time.

"What are you going to suggest?" Ancella asked. "That I should be your Receptionist?"

Sir Felix laughed.

"My waiting-room is far too crowded already without filling it with all the *jeunesse dorée* of fashionable Society! There would be more men consulting you than women consulting me, and that would be very bad for my morale!"

Ancella gave a little laugh which, however, turned into a cough.

She got out her handkerchief and choked into it for a moment or two while Sir Felix watched her.

When she was ready to continue, he said:

"I noticed that cough of yours last time I was here. It comes from being over-tired and spending a very long exhausting winter in this abominable climate."

"Are you suggesting I should swim to the South Seas?" Ancella enquired.

"No, I am suggesting that you should go to the South of France!" Sir Felix replied.

Ancella laughed again.

"Now you are treating me like one of your fashionable beauties," she said, "to whom you prescribe a sea voyage on a yacht with oysters and champagne every day or a Villa in the South of France with nothing to do but smell the mimosa and watch the bougainvillaea coming into bloom!"

"The latter is exactly what I am suggesting," Sir Felix said. "But actually you would have something to do."

Ancella looked at him with wide-eyed surprise.

"I had a letter yesterday," Sir Felix explained, "from a colleague of mine who is the most fashionable Doctor in Monte Carlo. He was reporting on a patient I sent him and at the end of his letter he wrote . . ."

As Sir Felix spoke, he drew a folded sheet of writing-paper out of the inside pocket of his coat and read aloud:

"I suppose you do not know of a Nurse, by any chance, preferably a lady, who could attend Princess Feodogrova Vsevolovski? Her Highness is as tough as a horse, but she thinks she needs a Nurse to trail around after her. I have no qualified Nurse whom I can possibly spare, and quite frankly the Princess needs no nursing. It is fashionable here to pretend one is an invalid. If you can think of anyone – and money is no object – it would, my dear Sir Felix, be of inestimable benefit to me, because these women are driving me mad with their incessant and unnecessary calls and I never have a moment to myself!"

Sir Felix, as he finished reading, folded the letter and said:

"Well, Ancella, what do you think of the idea?"

"A Nurse! But I am certainly not qualified."

"Dr. Groves says no qualifications are necessary and I imagine it is really a post as Companion. Could you bear to take on another elderly person – this time a *malade imaginaire*?"

"I really do not know what to answer," Ancella replied a little helplessly.

"I am not only thinking of the money, which Dr. Groves says is no object," Sir Felix said, "although I am quite certain, knowing a little of your father's affairs, it would not be unwelcome. I am really thinking of your health."

"Of my health?" Ancella repeated with a startled look in her eyes.

"You have had over a year of constant anxiety, tremendous pressure, and having to work far harder than any trained Nurse would have done," Sir Felix replied. "You have lost weight, Ancella, and quite frankly I do not like that cough! However I feel sure that a few months in the sunshine will disperse it."

He paused and went on:

"I also think living in a rich household you would eat more sensibly; for I have an idea that any small luxuries that came into this house went straight upstairs to your father's bed-room."

"You know quite well there has been no money for any extravagance," Ancella said.

"You really reinforce my argument," Sir Felix went on. "Why not be brave, Ancella, and try out this little experiment? After all, if the position proves really intolerable you can always come home."

"That is true," Ancella murmured, "but . . . Monte Carlo!"

"Does it sound such a frightening place in your ears?" Sir Felix asked. "I was there last year and I enjoyed it enormously."

"It has always been held up to me by my aunts as a kind of Sodom and Gomorrah," Ancella answered. "You know that Papa gambled away some of his inheritance when he was a young man? They have never forgotten it! They talk as if it happened only yesterday and they are continually preaching to me about the evils of gaming."

"I am not suggesting you should throw your hard-earned salary – and I have no doubt it will be hard-earned – on the tables!" Sir Felix laughed. "What I am suggesting is that you should get as much sunshine as possible, eat as much as you can stuff into your body and, when you look like you did a year or so ago, come back, and we will find a suitable husband for you!"

"Sir Felix!"

Ancella knew he was teasing, but she could not help the colour coming into her face.

"You talk as if I was longing to get married!"

"You have not had much chance so far," Sir Felix said dryly. "Tell me when you last went to a party, when you last danced a waltz."

"You know very well the answer to that," Ancella replied.

"Yes, I do, and I deplore it very much," he said. "You are very lovely, Ancella! I have admired you ever since you were a small child, and you are very like your mother."

Ancella gave a deep sigh.

"Mama was really beautiful!"

She was still for a moment. Then she said:

"Perhaps if she could have gone into the sunshine instead of suffering so abominably from the cold, she would have lived longer."

"That is why I am not going to let history repeat itself," Sir Felix said. "I want your permission, Ancella, to write to Dr. Groves to-night to tell him I have found the perfect person for his Princess."

"She must be Russian."

"The South of France is full of Russians," Sir Felix answered. "There are Grand Dukes, all handsome and attractive, throwing thousands of pounds away on the green-baize tables, building colossal Villas and entertaining most beautiful and delectable ladies of every sort and description!"

His eyes twinkled as he spoke, but Ancella said:

"I shall look a drab little English sparrow amongst such birds of Paradise."

Then she added quickly:

14

"But of course I shall only be an on-looker of the social world – not a part of it!"

"I am sure you will look very lovely whatever you wear," Sir Felix said consolingly.

"There speaks the eternal man who thinks that clothes do not matter to a woman," Ancella said mockingly. "But I dare say that as a Nurse-Companion I shall look suitably demure and no-one will notice me."

Sir Felix privately thought that that was most unlikely, but as he did not wish to alarm Ancella he said nothing.

Instead he rose to his feet, remarking:

"I must now return to London. I expect you have sent telegrams to your nearest relatives and one or two of them at least will be arriving during the afternoon . . . They will help you with the funeral, but I have already instructed the local Doctor to make arrangements with the Under-takers and not to trouble you more than is absolutely necessary."

Ancella rose too.

"Thank you again, Sir Felix," she said. "I do wish my relatives were like you! Because I love you, besides being so grateful for all you have done for Papa, I will do as you suggest. At least it will be an adventure!"

"It will indeed," Sir Felix agreed, "and I promise you that if you find the situation intolerable, you have only to telegraph me and I will either send you the money for your return ticket, or come and fetch you myself!"

He smiled and added:

"That would at least be an excellent excuse for me to revisit the Riviera, which I would very much enjoy!"

* * *

It was three weeks later when Ancella found herself travelling in the Paris-Lyon-Méditerranée Express, away from the cold snow and the bitter winds of the north, to-wards the Côte d'Azur.

Even now she could hardly believe that she had been able to get away instead of being coerced and brow-beaten by her aunts into going to stay with them rather than leaving England.

She had not told them, of course, what she was about to do, for she and Sir Felix had decided that would be asking for trouble.

Instead she pretended that she had been invited to stay with a friend in the South of France and had decided to accept the invitation.

They put all possible objections in her way.

It was too soon to stay away when she was in mourning! Such gadding about was unbecoming in a young girl who had recently been bereaved! It would be extremely improper for her to travel alone! And most important of all — she was not old enough to be without the constant chaperonage of someone like themselves!

As that, of all the arguments they reiterated over and over again was what Ancella most wanted to avoid, it made her more and more determined to escape.

She had already decided with Sir Felix that she would not call herself by her real name.

After all, the Winns were a large family, and although the Earl of Medwin had been too ill to go out and about ever since Ancella had grown up, there still might be some distant cousin or perhaps a friend who would recognise the name Ancella Winn.

"I will call myself Winton," she told Sir Felix. "It is no use inventing a name too unlike my own, or I shall never remember to answer to it!"

Accordingly Sir Felix had sat down and written to Dr. Groves that a Miss Ancella Winton would accept the post with Princess Feodogrova Vsevolovski and would arrive at Beaulieu Station on the 7th February.

Ancella had to tell her aunts that her friends lived near Beaulieu and this caused another storm.

16

"Beaulieu cannot be very far from Monte Carlo!" Aunt Emily exclaimed. "I can only hope, Ancella, that you will not contemplate for one moment entering that cesspool of wickedness!"

"I cannot believe it is as bad as that!" Ancella answered, remembering what Sir Felix had said.

"The dear Bishop has written several letters to *The Times* protesting against the wickedness of gambling," Aunt Emily replied, "and the misery that it brings to those who participate in such evil."

"People do not *have* to gamble, Aunt Emily," Ancella retorted.

To reinforce the argument her aunt had sent home for a scrap-book which arrived before Ancella left Medwin Park.

In it she had collected through the years pressed flowers, Ball programmes, Christmas messages, sketches and photographs, and had stuck them all into a scrap-book which she had entitled: *Mementoes of my Life*.

She turned over the pages and found a letter that had been written some years before by a man called John Addington Symonds, one of the earliest English visitors to Monaco.

His letter had appeared in a newspaper and Aunt Emily had cut it out. Part of it said:

"There is a large house of sin blazing with gas-lamps by night, flaming and shining by the shore like pandemonium or the habitation of some romantic witch . . . The witch herself holds her high court in the neverending festival of sin in the hall of the green tables . . . Splendid women with bold eyes and golden hair and marble columns of imperial throats are there to laugh, to sing songs, to tempt . . . Inside the gaming-house play goes forward like a business. *Roulette* and *Rouge et Noir* tables are crowded. Little can be heard but the monotonous voices of the croupiers, the rattle of gold under their wooden shovels and the click of the ball spinning round for roulette . . . The Croupiers are either fat, sensual cormorants or shallow lean-cheeked vultures or suspicious foxes. These men of the gaming bank show every trace of dissolute youth in a vile calling of low, sensual and hardened avarice upon their faces."

Ancella's aunt had read aloud in a low, shocked voice, and now raising her eyes and taking off her pince-nez she asked:

"You understand? That is what you must avoid!"

With difficulty Ancella prevented herself from laughing.

"I think you have forgotten, Aunt Emily, how hard up I am! Papa, as you well know, was unable to leave me any money. I have only £100 a year which my grandmother left me, and I assure you that that sum will leave nothing over for wild gambling."

"You are not to go inside that dissolute place. Do you understand, Ancella?"

"Yes, Aunt Emily."

"If anyone invites you to do so, you are to refuse. If the dear Bishop learnt that my niece had been seen in Monte Carlo I think I should die of shame!"

"I will try not to make you do that, Aunt Emily!"

"So I should hope!" her Aunt replied.

The cutting Aunt Emily read out had been written, Ancella knew, years ago.

Even so, she remembered there had been letters recently in *The Times* attacking Monte Carlo.

One of her duties had been to read to her father anything that might interest him in the newspapers, and she remembered a letter in the *Pall Mall Gazette* in which a Doctor who lived in Menton had said:

"I have several times had the mortification of seeing patients sink into graves who would have recovered had they not been enticed into one of the most pernicious forms of all excitements – gambling . . . The removal of this great evil from the beautiful shores of the Riviera would certainly be a benefit to our fellow-men and advance our Saviour's Kingdom."

"Damn nonsense!" the Earl of Medwin had exclaimed when she read the letter to him.

Another letter Ancella read aloud said:

"What of the suicides at Monaco – deaths registered as accidents but which would be more truly described as 'Murdered by Monte Carlo'?"

"Gross exaggeration," the Earl growled.

"But I saw in *The Times* yesterday, Papa," Ancella answered, "that a petition signed by four thousand residents and visitors to the Riviera has been presented to the French Chamber. It said that Monaco had become a 'den of corruption' and begged the French Government to put an end to the Casino."

"Blasted spoil-sports!" the Earl had ejaculated forcefully. "Why the devil they cannot live and let live I do not know! If people do not spend their money one way they will spend it another!"

He had dismissed the subject, but Ancella had found it impossible not to be curious about Monte Carlo and wondered whether it was in fact as evil as everyone made out.

The Daily News claimed that Queen Victoria, the King of Italy and the German Royal Family were anxious to put an end to the 'evil consequences of a hell such as Monaco'.

But the Earl would not listen.

'Perhaps now I shall have a chance to find out for myself,' Ancella thought as the train rushed through the night, carrying her towards what she described to herself whimsically as 'the beautiful and the bad'.

She was certain it was due to what Sir Felix had written to Dr. Groves that she was travelling, not as she had expected, Second Class, but First Class.

This enabled her to have a Sleeping Compartment, and she was fascinated by the small bed made up skilfully by the attendant, by the comfort of the washing facilities and by the fact that she could be alone.

She knew that when Society Ladies travelled they took with them their own silk or linen sheets, their lace-edged pillow cases, a mat on which to stand and every other adjunct which appertained to their comfort.

She could remember her mother describing to her how she and her father had travelled when they visited Europe.

They used to take with them a maid and a valet who packed and un-packed their luggage, made up their Sleeping Compartments, saw that everything in a train, a ship, a Hotel was arranged to their liking.

But although Ancella could not travel in quite such grand style she was not complaining.

She had been overcome when Dr. Groves had written back enthusiastically accepting Sir Felix's suggestion of sending him 'Miss Ancella Winton' and saying that he had persuaded the Princess to pay her the equivalent in francs of £150 a year.

"It is a fortune!" Ancella exclaimed when Sir Felix told her.

"You will find it will not go very far in the richest playground in Europe," he had answered. "So be sensible, Ancella, and remember that you must never spend any of your own money but always expect to be paid for."

"I hope I shall behave like a well-trained senior Servant!" Ancella laughed.

"Then remember that servants expect to be generously paid for their services and never in any circumstances to put their hands into their own pockets!" he said.

"I will remember," Ancella promised.

But because she felt she would be rich she had bought herself some new dresses.

She had not been extravagant but had bought, as her mother had always done, with taste and discrimination, which made every pound go a very long way.

She had already discussed with Sir Felix whether she should dress in mourning or whether her employer would find that irksome.

"Personally, knowing the Riviera, I think you will find that black is too hot and too gloomy," Sir Felix said. "There is colour everywhere and you will want to feel part of it."

Knowing he was speaking sound common sense, Ancella had purchased white and pale mauve dresses and had taken with her just one black evening-gown that she had bought after the death of her mother.

It had been rather an expensive gown, and as she had seldom worn it since then it seemed a pity not to make use of it now, even if it was only at dinner in the Villa, if by any chance she was asked to dine with her employer.

She did not really know what to expect, and there Sir Felix could not help her.

She did not know whether she would actually be treated as a senior Servant, expected to take her meals alone, or whether she would be invited into the Dining-Room.

'I shall just have to wait and see,' Ancella thought and told herself it would not matter either way.

What was really important was that she was getting away on her own and she was going into the sunshine.

Sir Felix had been astute in perceiving that she was extremely over-tired and run down.

Now that her father was dead she felt as if her main purpose in life had ceased, and all the exhaustion and fatigue that she had determined not to acknowledge while he needed her swept over her now like a flood-tide.

She was indeed very, very tired, and all she wanted was to have time to collect herself, to think about the future and plan quietly what she should ultimately do when this unexpected employment came to an end.

'I will save every penny of what I earn,' Ancella thought. 'I feel certain I shall need it when I come back to England.'

Again she thought of living with either of her aunts and shivered.

'It would be like deliberately walking into a tomb,' she told herself, 'and once there, there will be no escape.'

She fell asleep listening to the beat of the wheels, imagining they were a chariot carrying her from the darkness into the light.

'I am lucky,' she thought, 'so very lucky!'

It was early in the morning when Ancella awoke with a start to hear the porters shouting and to realise the train from Paris had reached its first stop.

"St. Raphael!" "St. Raphael!"

She heard the name and pulled up the shutters over her window.

For a moment the sunshine blinded her. Then she looked out onto the vivid blue of the sea, at a translucent sky which still held the misty haze of dawn and thought she was in Paradise.

Behind the small town there were mountains, their lower slopes richly wooded.

Ancella knew that it was in this little port that Napoleon landed on his return from Egypt in 1799 and embarked 15 years later for imprisonment on the island of Elba.

"I am living history!" she told herself ecstatically.

She dressed herself automatically, watching as she did so a new world unfolding itself before her eyes.

There were mimosa trees coming into bloom. There were flowers climbing up walls, filling window-boxes, and in the wild grass on the hill-sides. There were houses with vivid red roofs and white Villas which looked like iced cakes.

Far away in the distance she occasionally caught glimpses of mountain tops peaking high, still covered with the white snow of winter.

It was all so entrancing, so breath-taking, that she knew she had never before known colour to stir her emotions so strongly.

"It is wonderful! Wonderful!" she cried to herself and let down the window to feel the soft, warm air against her cheeks.

The train ran along the coast, stopping at places that had famous names.

Cannes, where Ancella knew the Prince of Wales often stayed, and which had a tempestuous past. Destroyed by the Romans as a punishment for the murder of some of their colonists, it was also twice destroyed by the Saracens.

The next stop was Antibes and Ancella saw displayed on the platform in varying shades of blue the urns, bowls and jugs which Sir Felix had told her were reviving the fame of the Roman Etruscan pottery.

Nice, she remembered was famous for its flowers and that Napoleon Bonaparte had had boxes of carnations, lilies, violets and roses despatched to him in Paris from there every week.

In the Bay of Villefranche were French and British warships lying at anchor off the shore, and Ancella heard a porter cry:

"Next stop Beaulieu!"

Hurriedly she collected her belongings and, taking a quick glance at herself in the mirror to ensure that she looked the part she had to play, she prepared to leave the train.

She had not been able to afford an expensive travelling-gown, but the one she wore, which was the purple of wood-violets, fitted her slim figure and made her look very elegant.

She had brought with her in a hat box some of the new straw hats which had been reasonably priced at Peter Robinson and which she had trimmed herself. But on her head she now wore a small bonnet trimmed with Parma violets in a paler shade of mauve than her gown.

'I hope I do not look too smart,' Ancella thought as she regarded her reflection, then smiled at her own conceit.

'All the richest and most beautiful women in the world come to the Riviera at this time of the year and I will certainly not compare very favourably with them!'

Since she had known where she was going she had taken a delight in turning up old copies of the *Illustrated London News* and the *Graphic*, which her father had always insisted were kept.

She found pictures of all the distinguished people who had Villas in the South of France; one magazine had told her that the Hotel de Paris had amongst its guests the Emperor and Empress of Austria, the Dowager Empress of Russia, the King of Sweden, the Queen of Portugal, and the King of Belgium.

'I doubt if I shall mingle with such famous people,' Ancella thought with a smile.

But she thought that she would like to look at them, especially the Empress of Austria, who was reputed to be one of the most beautiful women in the world.

"Beaulieu!" the porters were shouting as the train came into the station.

Ancella was standing looking out of her compartment window and one of the porters in his loose blue linen blouse signalled to her that he was for hire.

She nodded and raised her hand, and he stood outside the compartment window until the attendant let it down and handed Ancella's luggage out to him.

She had taken the trouble before she left for France to ask Sir Felix exactly what she should tip, and having changed some of her pounds at Calais she now gave the man a little more than what he expected and was rewarded with a '*Merci beaucoup, M'mselle!*'

She climbed down from the train onto the platform and just as she reached her porter a man wearing an elaborate livery came up to her and bowed.

"*Vous êtes M'mselle Winton?*" he enquired in French.

"*Oui,*" Ancella replied.

"Then will you come with me, *M'mselle*? Her Highness asked me to meet you and there is a carriage outside."

"Thank you," Ancella answered.

Sir Felix had told her she would be undoubtedly met.

At the same time she had been apprehensive that she would not be considered important enough, and guessing that the Villa might be some way from the station she had been wondering whether, when she reached it, she should pay the coachman if she hired one, or ask the servants to do so.

This answered her problem, and she found waiting outside a very comfortable carriage which to her delight was open.

The servant who had met her handed her in, and arranged the small pieces of her luggage on the seat opposite her, while her trunk was strapped at the back. Then he climbed up on the box and they set off.

The warm sunshine seemed almost like a caress on Ancella's pale cheeks.

Now that the sun had risen the sea was sparkling and she thought it impossible to imagine any part of the world could be more lovely.

The road was crowded with carriages and vehicles of all types. Some were very grand, the occupants being extremely elegant ladies holding up small sun-shades for fear of being sun-burnt.

Others were rough carts drawn by mules and to her delight Ancella often saw two white bullocks yoked together in harness.

Beaulieu seemed to have been built in a sheltered wood and there was a profusion of orange and lemon trees, tall hedges of roses and scented geraniums bordering it.

Above rose gigantic perpendicular cliffs, their skyline fringed with pine trees, the limestone interstratified with layers of red sandstone.

There were also magnificent ancient olive trees, some of them, Ancella had read in a guide-book, being over a thousand years old.

After leaving Beaulieu the carriage drove along the road known as the Lower Corniche. It had been hewn in some places out of the rock, and once they passed through a short tunnel so that Ancella's eyes had to adjust themselves from brilliant sunshine to partial darkness and back again to brilliance.

The railway-line ran beside them and before Ancella had progressed very far the train in which she had come from Paris passed them and she knew it was going on to Monte Carlo, which was the end of the line.

She knew that thirty years ago in 1868 it had been completed so as to reach Monte Carlo, and the effect had been explosive! Every day crowds of passengers poured out of the trains and into the gambling-rooms.

Ancella had noticed when they left Paris that the travellers on the express were very smart and opulent.

They certainly made themselves comfortable on the journey. She had seen huge hampers being carried in to their compartments or left outside, heard the 'pop' of champagne corks and in the morning had seen a great many empty bottles placed outside the doors, so that they could be cleared away by the attendants.

'How shocked Aunt Emily would be!' Ancella thought with a little smile.

Then suddenly the carriage turned off the road and began to descend a very steep drive-way which curved down the side of the cliff.

For the first time she realised that they had left the line of the railway and were between it and the sea.

When she had asked Sir Felix the address of the Princess Feodogrova's Villa he had told her it was the 'Villa d'Azar' – Point de Cabéel near Eza, and Ancella had looked it up on the map.

She had found it was a tiny promontory on the Monte Carlo side of Beaulieu.

It had been so small that it was only after searching for some time that she found it on a very large-scale map that her father had of all the different regions of France.

Now as the carriage curved down the tree-shaded drive, with the walls on either side brilliant with pink and crimson geraniums, she saw below her a large building with a flat roof gleaming very white against the green trees and the blue sea beyond it.

The carriage came to a stand-still outside an important-looking front door, on either side of which were pots containing coral-coloured azaleas.

The hall was spacious and cool, and a resplendent Major Domo bowed respectfully before he invited her to follow him.

Feeling for the first time a little apprehensive and nervous Ancella walked up a wide stairway.

On the first floor the Major Domo turned left and knocked on a closed door.

It was opened by a grey-haired maid with what Ancella thought privately was a disagreeable expression.

"The *M'mselle* from England," the Major Domo said.

The maid looked at Ancella, then walked ahead, obviously expecting her to follow.

She opened another door, and now for a moment Ancella was blinded by the sunshine pouring in from windows on two sides of the room.

Then she saw that seated in an enormous silk-draped bed, propped up against a profusion of pillows, there was an elderly woman.

27

"So you have arrived!" a querulous voice said in English, but with a slight foreign accent. "And about time! I began to think you must have got lost on the way!"

Ancella approached the bed.

Now she could see its occupant clearly and could not help being surprised.

The woman sitting back against the pillows seemed very old!

Her face was deeply lined and looked the texture of ancient Chinese parchment. There were, however, patches of rouge on her high cheek-bones and her lips were vividly coloured.

On her head was obviously a dark wig in which several diamond stars were glittering in the sunshine.

The glitter was echoed by the bracelets on her thin wrists and the rings on her fingers. Around her neck there were ropes of magnificent pearls so large as to look like birds' eggs.

Over her shoulders she wore a stole that Ancella knew was made of priceless Russian sable, and an ermine cover had been thrown aside on the bed.

She was so surprised at the Princess's appearance that for the moment she could find nothing to say.

The Princess might be old but her eyes were shrewd and as Ancella entered she looked her up and down, taking in every detail.

"So you are Ancella Winton," she said after a moment. "You are younger than I expected!"

Ancella felt a little guilty.

Sir Felix had deliberately abstained from mentioning her age, because he was afraid that Dr. Groves might think her too young to occupy such a responsible position.

"We will not lie," he had said to Ancella, "but we will not offer any unsolicited information. After all, only I know how experienced you are in nursing a sick person

28

and how extremely efficient you are under the most difficult circumstances."

"I am sorry if Your Highness is disappointed," Ancella
said, finding her voice after a distinct pause.

"I have not said so, have I?" the Princess snapped. "I
like young people, if they keep their place and if they know
how to behave!"

"I hope I shall do that," Ancella said.

"You are pretty – too pretty for this sort of employment," the Princess remarked. "Why are you not married?"

Ancella had an overwhelming desire to laugh.

This was not at all the way she had expected the inter-
view to take place between employer and employee.

"No-one has asked me!" she answered and saw the
Princess's lips twitch as if she was amused.

"Then you must have been shut up in a Convent or
incarcerated in a prison!" she remarked. "Have you had
breakfast?"

"I had a cup of coffee on the train," Ancella replied.

"Then you will be hungry!"

The Princess rang a small gold bell which lay beside her
on the bed.

Instantly the door opened and the maid appeared.

She was there so quickly that Ancella could not help
suspecting that she had been listening.

"Give *Mademoiselle* Winton something to eat!" the
Princess commanded, "and after she has unpacked and
changed her clothes, I will see her again."

The maid nodded. She was obviously a woman of few
words.

Ancella curtsied and went from the room, conscious
that the Princess's eyes were following her.

The maid led her across the landing at the top of the
stairs to the other side of the Villa.

There were a number of rooms here which the maid walked past until finally she opened a door, and Ancella saw a small room where the window looked out onto the other side of the promontory.

At a glance she could see that she could look back towards Beaulieu and the peninsula of St. Hospice at Villefranche, jutting out into the sea.

It was very lovely, so that with an effort she forced herself to turn to the maid and say:

"When I have unpacked and changed, shall I come to Her Highness's room?"

The maid nodded somewhat condescendingly and walked away.

"She is jealous!" Ancella told herself.

She knew that all lady's-maids hated Nurses or any other outsider who should somehow diminish their authority where their employer was concerned.

'Perhaps she will get to like me better later on,' she thought and because she was alone turned again to the window.

She had only just reached it when there was a knock on the door and two footmen came in carrying her belongings, and with them an elderly man.

She knew at a glance that he was Russian and he was in fact very ugly and strange-looking with a large, bald, egg-shaped head, high cheek-bones and deeply hooded eyes.

He appeared to be in charge of the footmen, giving them directions, but he looked all the time at Ancella and she felt he was sizing her up – looking her over in a manner she resented and felt was extremely impertinent.

The footmen unstrapped her trunk and then, as they straightened themselves, the Russian said in French:

"You have everything you brought with you, *M'mselle?*"

His voice was harsh and Ancella knew when he spoke there was something unpleasant about him.

"Everything, thank you," she replied coldly.

"If you want anything – ask me! I am Boris!"

"Thank you," Ancella replied.

She met his eyes deliberately, feeling in some way she could not explain that he was trying to intimidate her.

For a moment they looked at each other, then Boris turned away.

He preceded the two footmen out of the room and one of them shut the door.

"What a horrible man!" Ancella told herself.

She did not know why, but she felt there was something ominous about him – something dangerous for which she had no explanation.

Chapter Two

When Ancella had changed her gown and helped the French maid who came to do her unpacking arrange her clothes the way she wanted them, she went back along the corridor towards the Princess's room.

When she reached the outer door and knocked, it was opened by the old maid.

She looked at Ancella so aggressively that she explained:

"*Madame la Princesse* asked me to return when I was changed. I think she wants to see me."

"She's busy!" the maid said sharply, speaking for the first time since Ancella had arrived at the Villa.

She had a provincial French accent with an over-tone so that Ancella had the idea that she must have been with the Princess for a long time and perhaps spent many years in Russia.

She knew it was usual for the Russian aristocracy to have French maids, French tutors for their children, and when they were *en famille* to speak French.

In fact French was the *chic* language in St. Petersburg and she had not been apprehensive about communicating with her employer as she journeyed to France because she was quite certain that the Princess would automatically speak French, not only with her but also with her own relations.

She had, however, underestimated the linguistic skills of the Russians: that the Princess spoke excellent English was something Ancella told herself now that she might have expected.

Her father had told her that the Russians were a very cultured people.

"They may have been uncivilised in dealing with their serfs and the poorer classes," he said, "but those who can afford it are extremely well-educated and are men and women of great culture."

Ancella had never met a Russian before and the more she thought about the Princess the more fantastic she appeared.

Never had she imagined that a woman could wear so much and such magnificent jewellery and now she realised that the Villa itself was the height of luxury.

Even the furniture in her bed-room seemed to consist of museum pieces, and she had noted in the Princess's room, in the hall and in the corridor magnificent examples of Boulle and marquetry while she was sure the pictures on the walls were masterpieces.

She hoped she would have time to examine them more closely later on.

Now she said to the maid:

"Shall I return to my room?"

"No, wait, *M'mselle*," the maid replied. "*La gitane* will not be long."

Ancella's eyes widened.

'*La gitane*' meant 'the gypsy', and she thought she must be mistaken.

How could it be possible that the Princess was engaged in her bed-room with a gypsy? They were, she knew, considered out-casts in France as they were in Spain and many other European countries.

The old maid saw her surprise.

"You'll learn that there's nothing more important than *la chance*!" she said in a grumbling tone.

"The Princess gambles?" Ancella asked.

"You'll learn!" the old maid said again.

Ancella felt ashamed to be gossiping with a servant. At

the same time she was intensely curious.

"Will you tell me your name?" she asked in her soft, gentle voice.

"Maria!" the maid replied.

Ancella smiled.

"Then I hope, Maria, that you will help me. I have never been employed in this capacity before, and I am sure I shall make a great many mistakes without your guidance."

The suspicion and aggressiveness in the old woman's face melted visibly.

"You're too young!" she said after a moment's pause.

"I know," Ancella agreed disarmingly, "but I shall grow older and I have to start somewhere."

She thought there was a faint smile on Maria's face as she said:

"You just have to do what Her Highness requires. That's all she'll expect from you."

"I shall certainly do that," Ancella replied. "That, after all, is what I am paid for."

Maria glanced at the closed door which led to the Princess's room. Then she opened another one.

"You can sit down here in my room, *M'mselle*," she said. "*La Bohémienne* will not be long. As soon as she gets her money she'll scuttle off!"

"Does the Princess always consult her?" Ancella asked.

"Her, and a lot of other charlatans," Maria replied. "They're harpies, the lot of them!"

She spoke with so much disgust in her voice that Ancella wanted to laugh.

Just as she was about to question Maria further, there was the tinkle of the Princess's golden bell and the old woman went to the door.

Ancella saw a dark gypsy-woman, wearing jangling golden chains and huge ear-rings with a red handkerchief over her hair, being shown out onto the landing where Boris was waiting to take her downstairs.

She looked far too opulent and well-dressed to be the type of vagrant gypsy that Ancella had seen at home when they passed through Windsor, many of them journeying to the hop-fields of Kent.

As a child she had been fascinated by their dark eyes and black hair, their piebald horses and colourful caravans, but she had always been warned about them and threatened by her Nurse that they would kidnap her and take her away.

She had not believed that, since they always appeared already to have far too many children of their own, but she had realised that they were a strange and alien people.

She knew too that the villagers were afraid of them, not only attributing the loss of poultry to them as they passed through the countryside but also putting down to 'The Evil Eye' any illness arising in the months after their departure.

Ancella wondered whether *la gitane* had given the Princess really good advice.

She was quite certain that if Her Highness won she would attribute it to the gypsy's powers of divination and if she lost, the excuse would be that the planets were not favourable or the time of day unpropitious.

"Her Highness is ready for you now, *M'mselle*," Maria announced and Ancella rose from the chair on which she had been sitting, to walk into the bed-room.

The Princess was still in bed, but now, lying on the exquisite and obviously very valuable lace cover there were pieces of paper, astrological charts and a pack of worn cards.

The Princess regarded her with her bright, shrewd eyes.

"Have you ever played Baccarat or Roulette?" she asked.

"They are illegal in England," Ancella replied.

"I know that!" the Princess snapped. "But they are played in private houses and by your Prince of Wales."

"Yes, that is true," Ancella agreed. "I had forgotten."

"I do not suppose you have ever been invited to such parties," the Princess conceded. "What are your parents like? Very respectable?"

"My parents are dead!" Ancella said gently. "But Your Highness is right – they were very respectable!"

"And they would turn in their graves, I suppose, if they thought you were *une habituée* of the Casino in Monte Carlo?"

Ancella smiled.

"My aunts would certainly be scandalised!"

"Then it is fortunate they will not know," the Princess said, "for that is where you will be this evening!"

"*I* will?" Ancella exclaimed in surprise.

"I expect you to accompany me," the Princess replied. "Every night after dinner I visit the Casino and I play for two or three hours. As it is inconvenient trying to reach the table from a wheel-chair, I shall want you to place my stakes for me."

"Yes, of course, Ma'am," Ancella agreed.

At the same time she could not help feeling how horrified Aunt Emily and Aunt Edith would be if they knew.

"I wonder if you have the eye of Divination?" the Princess said reflectively. "Petula, the gypsy, who was here just now said I would meet someone with the eye. Do you think that is you?"

"I have no idea, Ma'am," Ancella replied.

"I suppose she was speaking of a man," the Princess said almost to herself, "but it might be you – it might be!"

"How does the gypsy predict your fortune?" Ancella asked.

"By cards and a crystal ball," the Princess replied. "But there is an astrologer – I think he is better than Petula – who works on my horoscope and tells me what will happen from the position of the stars."

The Princess paused for a moment, then said:

"It all comes back to luck. It is luck which counts, and I have never found anyone yet who could predict really accurately how luck would affect the turn of a card or the fall of the Roulette ball."

Ancella was quite certain this was true, but for the moment she was rather overcome with the idea that she should go with the Princess to the Casino.

She knew now that was what she wanted to do.

She had hoped against hope that being so near to Monte Carlo she would be able to visit the famous Casino which caused so much controversy and, if rumour was to be believed, tempted men and women to throw away their entire fortunes.

It seemed incredible that they should be so foolish, and Ancella thought perhaps it was just an advertising stunt.

When Aunt Emily and Aunt Edith had inveighed so fanatically against Monte Carlo, Ancella had read its history.

She had been entranced by learning how an arid plateau, pock-marked with troglodyte caverns and dotted with sparse, withered olive trees, had become within twenty years the most valuable piece of land in the whole of Europe.

The eight square miles of Monaco had certainly focused the attention of every civilised Capital upon its way of life.

It was not surprising, Ancella thought, when Monte Carlo was the only place where the rich, the important and the notorious could legally and publicly gamble.

She told herself she should be more interested in the ancient history of the Principality and the legend that it was used by sailors from the Greek colony of Marseilles who gave it the name Monoike.

It had also been patronised by the Phoenicians, who always planted palm-trees wherever they went.

The Romans had left behind ruins of some magnificent buildings which Ancella hoped to see, and she had learnt it was in Monaco that Julius Caesar assembled his Fleet before giving battle to Pompey the Great.

All these things had seemed to her fascinating in England, but secretly she had wanted to see the Casino itself, which had been opened in 1861 by the Monsieur François Blanc.

Living initially on a razor-edge of financial insecurity the Casino began slowly, then gradually became more and more successful until it attracted to Monte Carlo the most famous people in the world.

"I suppose you have an evening-gown?" the Princess asked sharply, breaking in on Ancella's thoughts.

"Yes, of course, Ma'am."

"Most people want to look their best in Monte Carlo," Her Highness said.

She chuckled and added:

"Except your Prime Minister, the Marquis of Salisbury, who has a magnificent Villa not far from here. He was turned away from the Casino the other afternoon because he looked so disreputable!"

Ancella laughed.

"I have heard that Lord Salisbury is very absent-minded and badly dressed. My father often spoke of him. At the same time he is a very great man."

"All men are great when they get to a position of power!" the Princess said.

She paused and added as if she spoke to herself:

"Power! That is what a man wants, and it is usually a woman who prevents his achieving it!"

There was a note of bitterness in her voice which Ancella did not miss.

As if following her train of thought the Princess rang the bell.

Maria appeared immediately.

"Where is His Highness?" the Princess asked.

"I told you, but Your Highness must have forgotten,"

Maria replied. "There is yacht-racing to-day."

"Yes, yes, of course!" the Princess said. "Have they all gone with him?"

"The Marchioness has," Maria answered, "and that jaunty friend of hers, Captain Fredrick Sudley. I don't know about the other gentlemen or Baron Mikhovovitch."

"I know where he is," the Princess said. "I was just wondering about the others."

"His Highness said he would not be back until this afternoon, so you had best have your luncheon and a good rest. You'll need it if Your Highness is going to play late to-night."

"How do you know I am going to play late to-night?" the Princess enquired.

"Does Your Highness ever do anything else after having listened to that gypsy woman?" Maria asked scornfully. "Filling you up with a lot of nonsense – that's what she's doing! If you ask me, it's an easy way to earn a louis!"

"I have not asked you!" the Princess retorted fretfully. "But I am certainly hungry, Maria. Tell Boris to bring my food here and a tray for Miss Winton. I am tired of eating alone."

"Will you tell His Highness that when he returns?" Maria asked.

She spoke with the familiarity of an old and valued servant, and Ancella had the impression that the two women enjoyed sparring with each other.

At the same time she wondered who the Prince was and whether he was the Princess's husband, or her son.

She was to learn the answer a moment later.

"Children are all the same!" the Princess exclaimed. "Selfish to the core! Thinking only of themselves! Vladimer knows quite well that I like him to be here for meals, but no! He goes off yacht-racing, on expeditions up mountains, excursions into Cannes, and I am left behind!"

"Perhaps he is afraid that it would tire you," Ancella

39

suggested, "if it is your son of whom you are speaking."

"Of course I am talking about my son!" the Princess replied.

Then her voice seemed to soften as she added:

"He is a good boy at heart, but too like his father – much too much like his father!"

Ancella could make no sense of this and she remained silent while the Princess muttered to herself, speaking first of Vladimer, then of Serge, which Ancella gathered after a time was the name of her husband who was now dead.

She glanced around the bed-room where there was every sort of ornament, *Objets d'art*, porcelain, carved ebonies and exquisite Fabergé boxes; but she could see neither a photograph nor a portrait.

It was fashionable to have photographs massed on every table, on a piano, on a writing-desk, and to carry them, as Queen Victoria did, from house to house and wherever she travelled.

But while the Princess's room seemed to be an Aladdin's cave of fascinating treasures, there were no photographs to help Ancella to know what the late Prince Serge looked like or to portray Prince Vladimer.

After luncheon the Princess, as if wishing to impress, showed Ancella her jewels.

Never had Ancella imagined that any woman could possess such a wealth of stones as emerged from the huge leather-covered boxes which Maria set down beside the bed.

There were tiaras that looked almost like crowns, fashioned of sapphires and diamonds, rubies, turquoises and pearls. There was one with emeralds so large that Ancella thought that if they were not worn by a Princess anyone would suspect them of being false.

Each tiara had a necklace, brooches, bracelets and rings to match. Each was more exquisite and more valuable

40

than the last, and they glittered in the sunshine until Ancella felt dazzled by them.

There were also sets of topaz and amethysts, and there were jade necklaces so old that they must have come from China when the British were still wearing woad.

There were ropes of pearls like the one the Princess wore round her neck, all glowing and translucent with the exotic beauty of the Orient, so that Ancella wondered what strange tales, if they could speak, they would relate.

The Princess soon grew tired of her jewels and returned to her horoscope and talismans, which she showed to Ancella as proudly as she had shown her jewellery.

There was a hare's foot and a lucky gold coin, the tooth of a whale, a piece of strangely shaped coral, the skin of a venomous snake, quite a number of silver medallions blessed by the Pope, and an eagle's claw.

The withered heart of a bat looked unpleasant, but the Princess told Ancella she had bought it for a very large sum from the relatives of a woman who had died of a heart-attack after breaking the Bank.

Ancella could not help thinking that the bat's heart had not brought its previous owner much luck, but she did not like to say so.

"What do you think this is?" the Princess asked, holding out a small piece of rope.

"It is obviously rope, Ma'am," Ancella replied. "Has it a very special meaning?"

"It was given to me by a Russian Colonel," the Princess answered. "It was part of a hangman's rope used at a mass-execution in Turkestan!"

"How horrible!" Ancella exclaimed before she could prevent herself.

"The Colonel told me it would bring me luck, but I doubt it!" the Princess said.

"Throw it away!" Ancella cried. "I am certain it is unlucky!"

"Why should you say that?" the Princess asked.

"Because I do not believe that anything that has brought death to one human being can bring luck to another."

Ancella thought for a moment that the Princess would be angry with her for speaking so positively, but instead she said surprisingly:

"Perhaps you are right! I will throw it away!"

She held it out, expecting Ancella to take it from her; but she felt she could not handle anything so horrible.

Instead she looked around, and seeing a waste-paper basket she carried it back to the Princess and waited for her to drop the piece of rope inside.

"I have a feeling you are not impressed by my lucky charms," the Princess said.

"I cannot believe they are any help," Ancella answered.

"You will see stranger ones when you are in the Casino," the Princess smiled. "There is one gambler – I know him well by sight – who has a match-box painted half red and half black. Inside there is a spider. When the spider tries to emerge from the red side its owner backs red, when it goes towards the black side he puts his money on black!"

Ancella laughed. She could not help it.

"That is ridiculous!"

"No-one will listen if you talk like that," the Princess said. "Many gamblers put a spoonful of salt in the pocket of their evening-coat to attract the right cards."

"How can they believe such nonsense?" Ancella enquired.

The Princess touched her bat's heart.

"If one wants to win," she said, "one will believe in anything!"

"You'll not have a chance of proving your luck tonight," Maria's voice said from the door, "if Your Highness doesn't rest!"

"Very well," the Princess said with a sigh. "Put my treasures away in my bag and I will try to sleep."

Ancella glanced towards the window.

"Would it be permitted for me to go into the garden?" she asked.

"Of course," the Princess answered. "This is your time off. You can do as you like. I shall not want you again until five o'clock, when I shall expect you to amuse me until we have to change for dinner."

"Do I dine with you?" Ancella enquired.

"You will dine downstairs and we will see what that woman is up to with my son!" the Princess replied.

She saw the surprise on Ancella's face at her words and asked:

"Have you not heard of that great English beauty, the Marchioness of Chiswick?"

"I do not think so."

"You will see her to-night and then you can tell me what you think of her."

"Now don't you start upsetting yourself over the Marchioness," Maria said. "From all I hear, she's just a guest in the Villa like everyone else. You don't have to worry about her."

"I know her type," the Princess muttered, "and do not forget, Maria, I was a beauty once myself!"

"You were indeed, Your Highness!" Maria said with a note of sincerity in her voice. "There wasn't a woman to touch you in St. Petersburg in the old days."

She put the big jewel-case away, and Ancella, feeling she was no longer needed, curtsied and went from the room.

As she went down the stairs she felt as excited as a small boy let out of school.

It had been so interesting listening to the Princess and she was fascinated by her. At the same time she knew she wanted to see the garden of the Villa and look at the sea.

There were several footmen on duty in the hall who bowed as she passed them. It was not difficult to find the way through the magnificent Salon and out onto the terrace which she had seen as she had glanced through the Princess's bed-room window.

Outside in the sun she realised that the Villa was built in a very unusual manner.

As it was against the side of the cliff, the ground floor was two stories higher than the garden and from the terrace outside the Salon, there was a flight of forty white marble steps.

On either side of the steps there were other rooms of the Villa built sheer against the rock, while the garden comprised the promontory of the Point de Cabéel, encircled with firs, olives and the wide-spreading glossy foliage of the carob trees.

Ancella remembered her father who was very knowledgeable on forestry, describing these trees to her and now, she thought excitedly as she walked down the marble steps, she could see one at close quarters.

She remembered now that he had said that Beaulieu and its vicinity were famous for the carob trees.

"They received their name from the Arabs who introduced them to the Riviera," he told her. "They were also called St. John's Bread as they are supposed to have supplied the locust-beans which formed the food of John the Baptist in the wilderness."

"How exciting, Papa!" Ancella said when he told her about it. "I would love to see the tree and eat its 'bread'."

The Earl had laughed.

"You would not enjoy them," he replied. "In Central Africa locust-pods are fed to mules and horses; but although they are sometimes eaten by human beings they are leathery and have a very disagreeable taste!"

On another occasion when he talked about the carob trees, he told Ancella that the husks which the swine ate in the Parable of 'The Prodigal Son' were undoubtedly the locust-pods of the carob and that was why they had been a punishment for the Prodigal's bad behaviour.

"What do you think he spent his money on, Papa?" Ancella asked. "Do you think he lost it gambling?"

Only Ancella would have dared to tease the Earl about an incident in his past about which he was extremely sensitive, having been nagged for so long by his sisters on the subject.

"I expect he spent it in the proverbial manner, on wine, women and song!" he replied. "But perhaps a portion of it was lost in the Eastern equivalent of Monte Carlo."

"I wonder what sort of games they played?" Ancella said, but her father could not enlighten her.

Now in the shade of the trees she walked towards the sea. On one side of the small promontory a high stone wall protected the garden, on the other side there was an exquisite view of the Bay of the Moors where the pirates from the Algerian coast used to land.

Above it rose the high cliffs climbing higher and higher to a sharp summit which she knew from the map was Eza.

The garden was filled with flowers and a fountain was playing in the centre of them. When Ancella reached the balustrade which bordered the sea, she looked back at the perpendicular yellow lime-stone cliffs behind the Villa.

Out of sight there was the famous, once dangerous, original Corniche road that had been the only way for travellers to journey from Nice to Monte Carlo.

There had been falls of rock, winds, cold from the snows of the Alps, to freeze them on their intrepid journey to Monte Carlo and brigands and robbers to relieve them of their winnings on their return.

'They must have felt it was all worth while as long as they could gamble at the tables,' Ancella thought.

The whole coast was so beautiful with tropical shrubs and trees growing down the cliff-sides and gorges, and she could see the soft green of grass interspersed with blue borage and the yellow and red of jonquils and anemones.

"How lucky I am!" Ancella told herself.

Then she leant against the balustrade and looked at the sea with its intermingling hues of emerald and sapphire and listened to the waves splashing below her.

Here was the Mediterranean, redolent with history, which had inspired poets, painters and writers since the beginnings of civilisation.

Ancella did not know how long she stood there, the music of the waves in her ears, while the scent of flowers in the garden filled the air with fragrance.

There were stocks, roses, hyacinths and azaleas, and she felt as if, together with the sunshine, they swept away not only her cough but also her worries and apprehension about the future.

It was as if such beauty held her in its arms and nothing could trouble her for the moment.

Suddenly a tuft of red sea-weed which had been flung by the waves onto the rocks below attracted her attention and made her bend further over the balustrade to look at it.

It was several feet beneath her and she wished she could collect it and hang it up outside her window to tell her, by whether it was moist or dry, what sort of day it would be.

Bending forward she must have dislodged the small cameo brooch she wore at the neck of her new lilac-coloured gown.

Ancella heard it tinkle as it fell onto the rocks and saw it lying not far from the sea-weed and just out of reach of the wash of the waves.

She stared at it frantically, then looked around to see if there was a gardener or anyone who could retrieve it for her.

She had very few pieces of jewellery and this brooch was one of her favourites because it had belonged to her mother.

Since there was no-one in sight and the garden seemed to be deserted, she walked along the balustrade to see if by any chance there were steps which could lead her down onto the rocks.

There were no steps, but Ancella saw an iron ladder attached to a small ancient turret which ended the protective stone wall and might at one time have been used as a watch-tower.

Looking round again to make sure that no-one could see her, Ancella picked up her skirts and, climbing over the balustrade, put her foot on the iron ladder and without much difficulty climbed down it.

As she reached the rocks she realised that the balustrade had been built out over them and she could walk in the shelter of it and be out of reach of the spray from the waves, although the rocks were in fact somewhat slippery.

Ancella was however a country girl used to walking and climbing, and although she was aware that if she slipped she might fall into the sea, she managed to creep along with her back against the rocks and to retrieve her brooch from where it had fallen.

She picked up the tuft of red sea-weed at the same time. It was the prettiest sea-weed she had ever seen, with tiny shells attached to it, and she was determined to take it back to the Villa.

Hidden under the balustrade she was looking at it when she heard voices and stiffened.

She felt it would seem somewhat strange if she disclosed herself at this moment: even the gardeners would think it unusual for a lady to climb down the iron ladder, and thereby reveal, had there been anyone to watch her, quite an improper amount of ankle!

Accordingly, her brooch in one hand, the sea-weed in the other, Ancella moved even further under the balustrade and kept still.

"I thought I would find you here," a man's voice said.

"I hoped you would have the sense to follow me, Freddie," a woman replied.

Ancella guessed that Freddie must be the Captain Sudley to whom Maria had referred so scathingly.

"I have been longing to talk to you, you know that," Freddie said. "Oh God, Lily, how long do we have to go on with this charade?"

"Until His Highness makes up his mind, I suppose."

Ancella told herself that the slightly affected, dramatic voice must belong to the Marchioness of Chiswick.

"Surely you can bring him to the point?" Freddie asked.

"It depends what you mean by that."

"Good Lord! You are not suggesting . . ."

"I am not suggesting anything, Freddie," the Marchioness interposed. "I intend to marry Vladimer and the sooner he realises it the better! But if it means that I must become his mistress first, then there will be no arguments on that score!"

"What do you think I should feel about that?"

"What you have always felt, I suppose – that I must have a rich husband and I am not likely to find anyone richer than the Prince."

"Blast his eyes!" Freddie ejaculated. "Why cannot I break the Bank for once in my life?"

"If you broke a dozen Banks, I doubt if it would last you long," the Marchioness replied in a tired voice. "You know as well as I do that money runs through your fingers like quick-sand, or whatever the expression is!"

"You do not hang on to it very long yourself, old girl," Freddie remarked.

"That is why I have to bring Vladimer up to scratch and as quickly as possible."

"I cannot think why he is being so slow about it," Freddie remarked. "He seemed keen enough in London."

"I think it is because his mother is here. I hate her and she hates me! That grotesque creature, Boris, repeats everything to her, I know. That is why we must be careful. I knew when I found him listening outside my door the other night that we must take no chances."

"That is all very well, Lily," Freddie said. "But if you think I can stand seeing you while unable to touch you, you are very much mistaken! If I do not have you to my-self I shall go mad!"

There was a note of passion in his voice which seemed to vibrate on the air.

There was a pause, then he added:

"Let me come to your room to-night. No-one will know."

"You are crazy!" the Marchioness said quickly. "It would spoil everything! I am quite certain that hob-goblin Boris sleeps with one eye open, and if he found out and told Vladimer, our plans would collapse with a bang, my dear Freddie! You know that is the truth!"

"I have a feeling that the Princess is the danger," Freddie said tentatively. "She is like a witch! She puts a spell on any woman her son fancies. So you had better be careful."

"What do you mean by that?"

"Look what happened to the girl he was engaged to."

"What did happen to her?" the Marchioness enquired curiously.

"She was found drowned – not here, but in another Villa they owned nearer to Monte Carlo."

"I do not suppose Vladimer really cared," the Marchioness said. "It was sure to have been an arranged marriage."

"I expect it was," Freddie said. "At the same time there was also a nasty accident to that dancer he was keeping. What was her name? Olga something."

"Olga Konveroski," the Marchioness said.

"Yes, that is right. I remember seeing her dance once. She really seemed to float across the stage."

"What happened to her?"

"She had an accident. She fell out of a window in St. Petersburg and broke her neck. The papers were full of it because she had just been such a success in Paris. You must have read the reports."

"I do not think they interested me," the Marchioness replied. "I did not know Vladimer in those days."

"Well, it is all in the past," Freddie said. "I do not mind saying I would have wagered my last sixpence that he would have proposed to you by now."

"I would have thought so too," the Marchioness agreed. "Oh, Freddie, if we do not bring this off, what shall we do?"

"Quite frankly I do not know!" Freddie replied. "Things are getting pretty awkward. If I go back to England, the bailiffs will be waiting for me."

"That reminds me," the Marchioness exclaimed. "I have something for you. Vladimer gave me a thousand francs to gamble with last night. I told him I had lost it but I have eight hundred for you. Take it out of my bag."

"Thank you, darling. It is jolly welcome, I can tell you. I am not spending a penny more than I can help while I am in the company of a Prince, but sometimes it is unavoidable. I have to pay for a drink sometimes or tip a servant in the Casino."

"Yes, of course you do! I know how difficult it is for you, but everything will be so different if Vladimer will only ask me to marry him. You could have polo ponies, a decent flat, anything you wanted, if I only had his money."

"Bless you!" there was a warmth in Freddie's voice which died away as he continued:

"It said in the papers that he gave that ballet dancer emeralds the size of postage stamps! It seems to me he is doing you on the cheap!"

"That is because at the moment I am neither fish, fowl nor good red herring! He has not asked me to be his wife or his mistress. Most men, my dear Freddie, even if they are Russians, do not pay up until the goods are delivered!"

"I hate your talking like that, Lily," Freddie said reprovingly. "I love you! You know damned well that I love you! I cannot bear to think of you belonging to another man."

"We have no alternative, do we? How long is it now since we fell in love with each other?"

"Ever since I first saw you when you were married to that boring old fossil," Freddie replied. "There should be a law against girls being married off to men old enough to be their grandfathers just because they are important!"

"He was a Marquis," the Marchioness said, "and after all, if I had been able to have a child, things would have been very different."

"I know! I know!" Freddie said irritably. "The Estate was entailed, provision being made for any child of the marriage, but nothing for the widow. The whole thing was damned unfair!"

"I still have a thousand a year!"

Freddie laughed and it was not a pleasant sound.

"It just keeps you in hair-pins, my sweet, and anyhow, you have mortgaged that about five years ahead!"

"Yes, I know," the Marchioness said helplessly, "but I do love you, Freddie! There has never been another man who makes me feel as you do! I suppose naturally I am a cold woman!"

"You are a one-man woman!" Freddie said sharply. "But when the one man has not a bean to bless himself with and his only qualification is an undistinguished Army career which he could not afford to continue, there is not much chance of our being happy together."

"But we will be!" the Marchioness corrected softly. "Once I have a rich husband!"

"That is what I am counting on," Freddie said.

There was a pause, then he added, with a deep note in his voice:

"Let me come to you to-night, my darling."

"We dare not! Vladimer is busy to-morrow with his yacht or something. We could take a drive into the woods at St. Hospice or up the hill."

"What use would that be with a coachman driving us?" Freddie asked crossly, "and doubtless a footman on the box?"

"We could go for a walk by ourselves and they would not dare to follow."

"Do you really mean that?"

"Of course I mean it! You know I want to be with you as much as you want to be with me – and Freddie . . ."

"Yes, my precious?"

"If I think it is safe I will come to your room to-night, but we shall have to be careful – very, very careful!"

"I shall be waiting for you – you know that. If only we could put 'knock-out drops' in Boris's drink!"

The Marchioness laughed.

"You must go back now. We have been here too long. I am quite certain we are being watched. We can only be thankful that no-one can overhear us here!"

"Yes, we must be thankful for small mercies!" Freddie said dryly. "Good-bye my darling, and thank you for the francs!"

"I will get you some more to-night if it is possible; but you will not gamble, will you, Freddie?"

"I cannot afford that sort of extravagance," he said almost savagely.

Ancella heard his footsteps as he walked away, but she dared not move, knowing that the Marchioness was standing just above her, leaning against the balustrade.

She must have stayed there for nearly five minutes before there was the sound of footsteps approaching and then a very different voice, deep and attractive, and with a charm which was entirely lacking in Freddie's, said:

"Why are you out here, Lily? I thought you would be lying down."

"It was so beautiful!" the Marchioness replied softly. "I am having such a lovely time, Vladimer, and I am so grateful to you!"

"I want you to be happy."

"Do you mean that?"

"Of course I mean it. Women who are as beautiful as you should never be anything else!"

"You say that too easily for it to be the personal compliment I hoped for!"

"You know you are beautiful! When you enter the Casino everyone turns to look at you. I thought last night you looked like one of the goddesses painted on the ceilings!"

"Dear Vladimer! You always make me feel as if I want to purr like a cat!" the Marchioness said. "May I return the compliment and say you are by far the most handsome and attractive man I have ever met?"

"Do you mean that?"

"You know I mean it!"

"Lily—"

There was something urgent in the way the Prince spoke her name.

"Pardon, Your Highness!"

It was a guttural voice that interrupted them.

"What is it, Boris?" the Prince asked in a slightly irritated manner.

"Her Highness asked me to tell you that she is awake and would like to speak to Your Highness before she starts to change for dinner."

"Tell Her Highness I will be with her immediately!" the Prince replied.

The servant must have bowed in acknowledgement for Ancella heard him moving away.

"I must go to Mama."

"Must you leave me? Our conversation was just beginning to be interesting!" the Marchioness said softly.

"We will continue it later," the Prince promised. "Will you stay here or will you walk back with me? I have a feeling you should be resting, so that you will dazzle them to-night even more effectively than you have done on previous evenings!"

"The majority of the men in the Casino would not raise their eyes from the tables to look at Venus de Milo!" the Marchioness laughed.

"They will look at you, just as I shall do," the Prince replied.

They must have walked away because Ancella heard their voices very faintly in the distance, then there was silence.

She realised she had been very tense as she stood listening, concealed beneath the balustrade.

Now she relaxed and moved tentatively over the slippery rocks towards the ladder.

She was intrigued and indeed fascinated by all she had heard.

Who could believe, she thought, that the Marchioness of Chiswick would behave in such a manner?

There was something positively unpleasant in the way she was trying to capture the Prince while at the same time being in love with Captain Sudley.

Ancella told herself it was ridiculous to be shocked. This after all was how she had always expected the fashionable world to behave.

There had been enough gossip and talk about the 'Marlborough Set' and their love-affairs.

Even living quietly with her father she had known that the Prince of Wales had been enamoured first with the exquisite Mrs. Langtry, then with Lady Brooke, and now with Mrs. Keppel.

There had been beautiful women who were talked about by others who were either envious, curious or shocked.

Sometimes the newspapers even hinted about liaisons which were well known to all Londoners, and which percolated slowly back to the country to be related to the Earl by his visitors when they wished to keep him amused.

Ancella had listened, but the scandals had not seemed to her to be particularly interesting because she did not know the people concerned.

Also the social scene had seemed very far away and utterly remote from her or her life.

But now, within a few hours of arriving in the South of France, she had stumbled inadvertently upon a social intrigue which not only surprised but also disgusted her.

"How could a lady behave in such a manner?" she asked herself.

She was also outraged at the idea of a man, who should be a gentleman, accepting money from a woman which she had obtained from another man.

Ancella climbed up the ladder and peeped over the balustrade to see if there was anyone in the garden. Then quickly, hoping she would not be seen from the Villa, she climbed back onto the terrace.

Carrying the piece of red sea-weed and her brooch she hurried back under the shade of the trees.

The water from the fountain was iridescent in the crimson and orange rays of the sun and she hoped that this would distract anyone from noticing her movements before she reached the Villa.

She had no intention of entering it by climbing the white marble stairs. Instead she walked up a path at the side of the building and found, as she had expected, a door which was open.

Inside Ancella moved along various passages until she found a staircase and climbed it, to find herself in the corridor where her bed-room was situated.

She went inside, shut the door and locked it. She wanted to think over what had happened, and she wanted to feel that for the moment she personally was safe from the intrigues that were taking place around her.

She walked to the dressing-table and opened the drawer in which she had put the leather box in which she kept her brooch.

As she did so she had a strong impression that someone had been in her room.

It was difficult to be certain, and yet she had the feeling that someone had examined her personal belongings and replaced them not quite in the same way as she had left them!

Who could it be? And why?

Chapter Three

As Ancella dressed for dinner she thought how incredible it was that she should be going to a big social dinner-party and then on to the Casino in Monte Carlo.

She thought, when her father died, that her life which had always been quiet and uneventful would continue even more so.

The only prospect in front of her until Sir Felix had come forward with his suggestion, was that she should live with one of her disagreeable and strait-laced aunts who thought any pleasure must be wrong simply because one enjoyed it.

She had never in her wildest dreams thought that she might travel to the South of France, and that she would only have to look out of her window to see the exquisite and breathtaking beauty of it.

'That in itself should be enough for anyone,' she thought.

But on top of it to know that she was about to visit the most sensational and controversial building in Europe and to see, and perhaps meet, some of the distinguished and notorious personalities of the time was incredible.

She had learnt from the Princess that, while there were a number of guests staying in the Villa, almost every evening friends joined them for dinner from the hotels or from the Villas nearby.

"But we shall be a small party tonight," the Princess said, "because my son has told me that he has been invited to dine with the Grand Duke Mikhail of Russia, to meet the Prince of Denmark. It is an invitation he cannot refuse, and therefore I must look after his guests and we shall meet later in the Casino."

"Does everybody go to the Casino in the evening?" Ancella asked.

"Everything that is amusing takes place in Monte Carlo," the Princess answered, "and one night, if I spare the time from the tables, we will attend the theatre."

"There is a theatre in the Casino?" Ancella exclaimed in astonishment.

The Princess smiled.

"It was built by Charles Garnier who designed the Paris Opera House," she replied. "There are just as many golden giants, golden naked boys and nubile slaves holding golden candelabra as there are in Paris!"

The Princess chuckled and said:

"They always tell the story of how François Blanc's wife, when she saw it, said acidly:

"'All this vulgar display of gilt will only serve to remind the customers how much gold they have lost at the tables!'"

"I would love to go to the theatre!" Ancella said.

"We shall have to see who is appearing," the Princess replied. "Last year I heard *Faust* and saw Sarah Bernhardt in some play – I forget the name."

She chuckled.

"The divine Sarah was very unfortunate at the tables."

"Was she wonderful on the stage?" Ancella asked.

"Some people thought so," the Princess replied.

She changed the subject and Ancella thought that having so generously made the suggestion of taking her to the theatre she was now regretting it.

Ancella was to learn at dinner that the theatre was not the only surprise she was to have about Monte Carlo.

Before she reached the dinner-table she had been very worried as to what she should wear.

She had, on Sir Felix's advice, bought white or lilac dresses for the daytime and two white gowns for the evening.

They had not been expensive, but they were very attractive although rather plain compared with the elaborate beruched and befrilled confections of tulle and lace, satin and mousseline, which were fashionable.

Ancella thought that her one black evening-gown would seem too sombre, but when she had put on one of her white gowns she thought that perhaps she looked too much like a débutante.

She had a sudden fear lest the Prince should think she was too young and inexperienced to look after his mother.

"Supposing," she said to herself, "he insists on sending me away and asks the Doctor to provide someone older?"

She looked at herself in the mirror and wondered what she could do to make herself look more responsible. Then she thought with a smile that no-one would in fact notice her.

After all, downstairs, one of the most beautiful women in England would be in the party, and who would notice or even wish to speak to 'Miss Winton', who was merely a Companion-Nurse to Her Highness?

However, she could not help seeing that her grey eyes looked very large in her small face, and her fair hair, 'paler than the dawn', picked up the lights coming through the window of the last dying rays of the sinking sun.

The gown revealed Ancella's tiny waist, there was soft chiffon draped around her white shoulders, and her neck was long and held her head proudly.

Because she wanted to relieve the white of the gown, she took two pale pink rose-buds from the flowers that were arranged on a table in her bed-room.

She pinned them in the bow on her breast and thought perhaps it made her look a little less *ingénue* and more sophisticated.

Once again she told herself that the important thing was that she should be as unobtrusive as possible, and went from her bed-room to find the Princess.

She was to learn as the evening progressed that the Princess could walk if she wanted to.

She was not so infirm that she could not walk about her rooms, and although she was carried down the stairs in a chair by two footmen she walked into the Salon and from there into the Dining-Room.

There were a number of people already assembled in the Salon, and even if she had not recognised the slightly drawling voice of the Marchioness of Chiswick, Ancella thought she would have known who she was because she was so beautiful.

Never had she imagined a woman could look more the living embodiment of a Roman Juno.

She was tall, even compared with the tall and statuesque beauties of the period like the Duchess of Sutherland and the Princess of Pless, whose photographs appeared in every magazine and were on sale as postcards.

Her hair was the vivid gold of ripening corn and her eyes so blue that they rivalled the Mediterranean.

She carried herself superbly and her gown revealed her full bosom above a small pinched-in waist and wide hips.

As the Princess entered the Salon the Marchioness swept towards her, curtsied and said effusively:

"Your Highness! We have missed you so much to-day! It was so sad you could not watch the yacht-racing. It was fascinating!"

"I am sure it was!" the Princess said dryly. "Especially if my son won!"

"But of course he won!" the Marchioness replied. "Is His Highness ever defeated at anything on which he sets his heart?"

There was something so ingenuous in the way she spoke, and she looked so fascinating as she did so, that Ancella found it hard to look round and decide which amongst a number of gentlemen, all extremely elegant with their white shirt-fronts and long tail-coats, was Captain Fredrick Sudley.

It was not difficult to distinguish him.

She heard his rather hard voice and loud laugh and saw that he was in fact good-looking with dark brown hair, a moustache and a manner of holding himself which proclaimed his military training.

It was difficult for Ancella to distinguish at first between the house-party and those who were guests for the evening.

She was introduced to Baron Mikhovovitch, and found later when he sat next to her at dinner that he was a charming, elderly man with a courtly manner who had once been in the Diplomatic Service.

In the Salon Ancella kept herself unobtrusively beside but a little behind the Princess, and while the Marchioness pointedly ignored her a number of the gentlemen either asked to be introduced or talked to her without waiting for an introduction.

"I must be very careful not to push myself forward," Ancella told herself, "or to do anything to attract attention."

She was quite sure that the Marchioness would be ready to snub her if she should do so, but she was not certain what the Princess's reaction would be.

The Princess sat at the top of the long table. Ancella found that while on one side she had the Baron Mikhovovitch who told her interesting things about Russia which she found fascinating, on the other she had a middle-aged man who was inclined to be flirtatious.

She had met his type before, and when she made it quite clear that she had no intention of responding to his rakish insinuations, he became tired of her and turned to talk to the woman on his other side.

The dinner was a surprise to Ancella, for living quietly

in the country she had never realised the luxury to be found in houses where a superlative Chef was employed.

Course succeeded course, each more delectable and more exotic than the last. She knew this was French cooking, as her father had described it to her, at its best.

She found it absolutely impossible after the first two courses to eat anything but the very smallest mouthful of each dish she was offered, but the gentlemen in the party ploughed through everything.

It was not surprising, she thought, that many of them had grown so fat in middle-age if that was the way they indulged themselves day after day.

There was champagne to drink and other superlative wines, which made Ancella wish that her father was there as she knew how much he would have enjoyed them.

She wondered if in her position she ought to refuse wine.

Then she told herself that it was unlikely in France that anyone would think it strange for her to drink what was offered, considering that even the poorest peasant had a bottle of *vin ordinaire* with his meal.

The conversation was gay and varied and Ancella noticed that the Marchioness held the attention not only of her partners at the dinner-table, but also of others in the immediate vicinity.

She was vivacious and, judging by the laughter, amusing. But when Ancella overheard some of the remarks she realised that they had a *double entendre* which she did not understand.

"How stupid I must seem to these people!" she thought, then told herself severely that she was talking as if they would judge her as an equal.

To them she was just a servant and, as long as she answered them politely when they condescended to speak to her, nothing else would be expected.

Baron Mikhovovitch told her he had been watching the tennis tournaments.

"Do they have them in Monte Carlo?" Ancella asked in surprise.

"Indeed they do! There are five women champions here who play magnificently. You must watch them."

"I would like to do that," Ancella exclaimed.

"If I were younger," the Baron said gallantly, "I would not only challenge you on the Courts, I would ask you to be my passenger in the first *Concours d'Elégance* for motor cars!"

"What is that?" Ancella enquired.

She had once or twice driven in a motor car belonging to a friend of her father's and found it a fascinating experience.

"The driver whose car is adjudged to look the most beautiful gets a prize and so does the lady who accompanies him."

"There must be a lot of competition."

The Baron laughed.

"Actually, no! Everyone is sure to get a first prize because there can never be anything second or third class in the Principality!"

Ancella laughed too.

"How reassuring!" she exclaimed.

As soon as dinner was finished, the Princess moved with the ladies from the Dining-Room and immediately wished to go to the Casino.

"There is no hurry, Your Highness!" someone remarked.

"Indeed there is!" the Princess replied. "I feel that tonight I am going to win!"

"Then good luck!" the gentleman said who had spoken to her. "I shall follow your lead. I lost a packet last night!"

"You are not a good gambler, My Lord!" the Princess said severely.

"Unlucky at cards – lucky in love!" he retorted and turned a roguish eye on Ancella as he spoke.

The Princess's carriage was the first to leave the Villa and Ancella was surprised to find that it was drawn by four horses.

As if in answer to a question she had not asked the Princess said:

"No reason to waste time in travelling to Monte Carlo. My horses will get me there quicker than anyone else!"

As the carriage moved off Ancella was aware that the Princess was in a somewhat agitated state of mind, and she knew that she carried with her in her black velvet bag almost all her lucky charms.

Looking at the Princess at dinner she had thought that never had she imagined any woman could wear so much jewellery or appear to be so rich.

The Princess literally blazed with diamonds: she wore a necklace that she had shown Ancella that morning, which consisted of three rows of diamonds each one as big in size as an English 6d!

"How can anyone already so wealthy want more money?" Ancella asked herself.

She began to think that perhaps the newspapers, when they talked of 'gambling fever' and 'an obsession which was detrimental to mind and health', were perhaps not exaggerating as much as she had thought at first.

She was however so fascinated by their destination that she could think of little else.

Very soon, because of the fast pace at which they were travelling, she could see the lights of Monte Carlo. Then as they entered the town she saw the harbour filled with large and expensive yachts, their lights gleaming in the darkness and reflected on the water beneath them.

It was very lovely, but there was no time for more than a passing glimpse before they were climbing the hill, until everything seemed to be ablaze with lights as the carriage came to a stand-still in front of a long flight of steps.

They had arrived!

There in front of them, Ancella saw, was the Casino with its two copper towers, looking exactly like the pictures she had seen of it – a large, fat, white-sugared wedding-cake.

At the appearance of the Princess's carriage two flunkeys who had been waiting at the top of the steps hurried down, carrying between them a wheel-chair padded with velvet which they set down on the pavement.

Ancella, who had seen the Princess walking quite adequately in the Villa could not help looking at it enquiringly, and the Princess, as if she read her thoughts, said with a smile:

"I assure you, my dear, when one is old, by far the most comfortable way to travel about the place is in a wheel-chair. Everyone gets out of the way and one is always the centre of attention!"

Ancella was amused, but she saw that what the Princess said was true; for as she was pushed through the huge, noisy gambling room everyone did in fact make way for her.

Ancella had a quick glimpse of a high, painted ceiling, a great deal of gold ormolu, a number of Roulette tables filled with people of all sorts and conditions crowded around them.

There were women with painted faces wearing huge hats covered in ostrich feathers or ospreys, there were poor clerks rubbing shoulders with well-to-do *bourgeoisie*, besides foreigners of every type, age and colour.

The Princess was swept past them, although Ancella longed to stop and look around to see what was happening.

"Faites vos jeux, Messieurs et Mesdames." "Les jeux sont faits." "Rien ne va plus."

She could hear the drone of the Croupiers' voices and

65

the sudden hush that came to a table as the wheel spun, but the Princess was being carried quickly ahead towards the *Salle Touzet*.

This room, she learnt later, had been added because the original gambling room now known as 'the Kitchen' had become so overcrowded.

It was carpeted with a floral design of dark and light blue, and attractive paintings hung on the panelled walls. Here the most distinguished and wealthy visitors to the Casino were encouraged to gamble.

In contrast to 'the Kitchen' the *Salle Touzet* seemed quiet, but Ancella felt that the atmosphere of excitement was even more tense, and it was in fact a very colourful scene.

Never had she imagined she would see so many beautiful and gorgeously-dressed women in one place.

They all wore evening-gowns and, while many of them wore diamonds in their hair, others sported Birds of Paradise or a profusion of ospreys and their gowns were very *décolletées*.

They literally sparkled with jewels, some of their necklaces, brooches and bracelets being almost as magnificent as those worn by the Princess.

It also seemed to Ancella that everywhere she looked she saw tall, good-looking, well-groomed gentlemen, many of them smoking fat cigars, others holding a glass of champagne as they either talked to each other or watched the turn of the wheel.

The Princess was conveyed across the room to what Ancella had already learnt was her favourite table.

The Croupiers greeted her respectfully and a place was made for her so that her wheelchair took the place of one of the twenty gold and red seated chairs, which was taken away.

There were, however, far more people standing than sitting and the Princess brought out a number of pieces of paper before she put notes to the value of 10,000 francs down on the table and demanded change.

"Four hundred pounds!" Ancella exclaimed to herself.

A huge pile of gold chips was pushed towards the Princess and now she was concerned only with the pieces of paper which Ancella had learnt before dinner had been given to her by her astrologer.

"To-night I shall follow the planets," the Princess had said, and when Ancella looked mystified she said sharply:

"Surely you realise there are numbers and symbols related to the laws of space?"

"No, Ma'am, I do not know that," Ancella answered. "Will you please tell me about it?"

The Princess had shown her charts and Ancella learnt that each planet had certain numbers which one should follow at the right time of the month.

"To-day we are in Venus," the Princess said. "That means that I must back 6 – 15 – 24 and 33. Although the sun has a certain amount of influence, which means I cannot ignore 1 and 4!"

It all sounded very strange to Ancella.

She tried hard to concentrate on what the Princess was saying to her but she could not help wondering privately how it could be possible that Saturn, Jupiter, Mars and Mercury could really influence the thirty-six numbers of the Roulette table.

However, the Princess undoubtedly believed it, and after studying her charts for some time she told Ancella to cover the numbers of Venus.

Ancella, picking up a chip for 20 francs, did as she was instructed.

"I wonder if you will be lucky for me?" the Princess muttered. "Let me see – what is the number of your name? Ancella is seven, Winton is six. That makes thirteen. Put 500 francs on thirteen. It might turn up! They say a woman always wins the first time she plays Roulette."

Ancella hesitated.

Surely, she thought to herself, there could be nothing in that superstition? At the same time, if it was so, the number she really should be on was eleven and not thirteen!

It was impossible of course to explain this to the Princess who had gone back to consult her charts and was ordering her to add 100 francs here and 100 francs there on the board, just as a protection.

"*Rien ne va plus,*" the Croupier said, his right hand on the wheel, the small white ball ready between his thumb and fore-finger.

He spun the wheel evenly and as the ball swung round the outside of the numbers Ancella suddenly knew quite clearly that number eleven would turn up.

As she had told Sir Felix, she sometimes had a conviction about such things and she was convinced without reason that the Princess would lose everything she had staked.

She was right!

The ball clinked into a slot, the Croupier brought the wheel to a stand-still, then announced:

"*Onze, noir impair et manque.*"

"Well your name certainly has not been lucky for me," the Princess said tartly.

"I am sorry, Ma'am."

"Now let me see what I do next," the Princess said rustling her papers, apparently quite unperturbed as the Croupier raked away every chip except those belonging to the few fortunate people who had backed number eleven.

The Princess gave her orders and Ancella carried them out.

It was uncanny and she tried not to listen to the inner voice which told her the number.

She looked round the table.

Everywhere she looked, the faces of the men and women gambling were hard and greedy.

There was something nauseating in the manner in which they watched, with every nerve of their bodies tense, the spinning of the Roulette wheel.

If they won, their hands went out almost like claws to clutch at their winnings, as if they were afraid they would evaporate in front of their eyes like fairy-gold.

Even some of the dinner-guests at the Villa, who had seemed charming, ordinary people, now looked to Ancella like vultures as they watched their money disappear.

Then, sullenly, their lips set in a hard line, they would move away to another table in search of better luck.

Ancella must have been obeying the Princess's instructions for nearly half-an-hour when a gentleman came to Her Highness's side and taking her hand from her lap lifted it to his lips.

"André!" she exclaimed. "I was not expecting you in Monte Carlo for another week!"

"I was able to leave Paris earlier than I expected," he said, "and how could I keep away when I knew you were here?"

The Princess laughed at him quite coquettishly.

"You know I have been looking forward to seeing you."

"And I you," he replied. "Stop losing your money and come and talk to me. There is so much I want to hear!"

Much to Ancella's surprise the Princess agreed.

She signalled to a flunkey, who pushed her chair away from the table towards an adjacent room where there were comfortable sofas and armchairs in which a few people were sitting drinking.

Ancella followed the Princess as she chatted away vivaciously to the new arrival. He was a middle-aged man with greying hair but still attractive, with a trim figure.

As the flunkey stopped the wheel-chair in front of a table and beside an arm-chair, the Princess suddenly seemed to remember that Ancella was there.

"This is my new Companion-Nurse," she said to the gentleman. "Miss Winton – the Comte André de Valpré."

Ancella curtsied, the Comte bowed.

"*Enchanté, Mademoiselle!*" he said mechanically.

"Vladimer will be looking for me," the Princess said, "and he will be surprised to find I am not in my usual place. Find the Prince, Miss Winton, and tell him where I am."

As the Princess finished speaking she turned towards the Comte, who had settled himself in the arm-chair beside her, and started to talk rapidly in an intimate manner which made Ancella feel it would be embarrassing to interrupt her.

At the same time, since the Prince had not been present at dinner, she had no idea what he looked like.

As she moved back into the gambling room she thought perhaps she could ask one of the many footmen in livery standing around and attending to the needs of the guests.

It was certain they would know the Prince and could point him out to her.

Then she hesitated, wondering how she could frame the question so that it would not sound as if she was seeking the Prince on her own account.

Then she saw the Marchioness of Chiswick and knew that the man talking to her had every likelihood of being the Prince.

There was something in the way in which the Marchioness was speaking and her caressing manner of putting out one white-gloved hand, which made Ancella sure that it was the Prince who was with her.

He was taller than she was and as Ancella walked towards them she could only see the back of his head and his broad shoulders.

At the same time his body was very slim and athletic, with narrow hips, which could not have belonged to an Englishman.

The Marchioness was looking up at him, her lovely face quite dazzlingly beautiful under the lights, and her lips seemed to be appealing to the Prince as if she was asking a favour of him.

As Ancella reached their side she felt shy and a little embarrassed because she must interrupt their conversation.

At the same time, she told herself, she must do as the Princess had ordered her to do.

She stopped still a little behind the Prince.

The Marchioness saw her and there was no mistaking the hard look that came into her eyes or the sharpness of her voice as she asked:

"What do you want, Miss Winton?"

"I have a message for His Highness, Prince Vladimer," Ancella replied.

She had not been mistaken. The man talking to the Marchioness turned round.

"For me?" he asked.

He was undoubtedly the best-looking and the most attractive man Ancella had ever seen!

Never had she imagined that any man could be so handsome and at the same time look so un-English.

She did not know what she had expected of a Russian Prince, but certainly not a man who looked like Prince Vladimer.

It was difficult to know why she should be so sure he was a foreigner; he was not in fact particularly dark and his eyes, like her own, were grey except that they had a touch of green in them.

It was perhaps the way his hair grew back from his oval forehead, or perhaps the straightness of his perfectly proportioned nose and the squareness of his chin.

Perhaps more than anything else his face was so expressive and his lips had a slight twist as if they were amused by life and yet cynical about it.

Ancella looked at him wide-eyed, unaware that she was staring and that he too was staring at her.

It seemed for the moment as if they met across eternity, that she had always known that somewhere in the world there would be a man like him.

She could not explain to herself what she felt. She just knew he was different from what she had expected, and from any other man she had ever seen before.

She felt as if the Casino was not there, and the Marchioness was not beside them, and they were alone and speaking to each other without words.

Then she heard the Prince say in the deep, attractive voice that she had listened to as she crouched on the rocks beneath the balustrade.

"Who are you?"

"This is your mother's new Nurse from England," the Marchioness interposed, and it appeared to Ancella that she spoke from a long way away.

"What is your name?" the Prince enquired, his eyes still on Ancella.

"Ancella Win ... ton, Your Highness!"

She stammered a little over the second syllable of Winton, feeling somehow she wanted to tell him the truth.

"Then I must welcome you to my household, Miss Winton."

The Prince's smile seemed to illumine his face and Ancella realised that he smiled not only with his lips but also with his eyes.

"Thank you," she said in a low voice and she curtsied, thinking it was something she should have done before.

"You have a message for me?" the Prince asked gently, as if he were prompting a nervous child.

"Yes . . . Her Highness asked me to tell you that she is in the Salon next door with a friend. She thought you might miss her at her usual table."

"I was just going to look for her," the Prince remarked.

"Your mother obviously does not need you," the Marchioness said before Ancella could speak. "Let us play Baccarat together. I am sure I shall bring you luck!"

"My mother may need me," the Prince replied.

He was still looking at Ancella, and as if she realised that his attention was not entirely hers the Marchioness said angrily:

"Do not be so ridiculous, Vladimer. If she is with a friend she will not require you. Come along – I want to see you break the Bank!"

Reluctantly, it seemed to Ancella, the Prince allowed himself to be drawn away by the Marchioness, who had slipped her arm through his.

They moved towards the other side of the room and Ancella stood for a moment watching them go, then turned to walk back towards the Princess.

She did not know why, but she felt as if she had experienced a kind of shock, something which had shaken her in a manner which she could not explain to herself.

She moved automatically across the room through the throng of people. She could see the Princess still deep in conversation with the Comte and felt that if she joined them she would certainly be *de trop*.

It was then she saw an open window, the curtains blowing a little from the breeze which came from outside, and, parting them, she walked out onto a terrace.

Instantly she was conscious of the magic of the night, the stars brilliant above her, the branches of the palm-trees silhouetted against the darkness, and below there was the sea.

She moved forward and saw the bowl of the harbour with its lighted yachts as she had seen them when they entered the town.

On the other side of it was a huge rock on which there was the outline of the Royal Palace where the Ruler of Monaco, Prince Charles, was guarded by an Army of ninety carabiniers wearing, Ancella had learnt from her guide-book, a uniform of blue and scarlet under a white helmet ornamented with a plume.

The sea-air was very soft and was not in the least cold, and mixed with the salt of it Ancella could smell the fragrance of night-scented stocks and lilies.

Somewhere, far away in the distance, there was the music of a band and she thought how romantic it was – a fairy-tale Capital made for happiness and yet it seemed impossible that the people struggling, striving and straining to win money at the tables could ever find it.

She walked a little further out into the garden, looking at the sea which seemed to gleam almost luminous in the reflection of the stars.

Then as she thought she should return to the Princess, she saw a man come through the window, as she had done, and fling himself down on one of the seats.

He gave a groan that Ancella could hear quite clearly. Then he doubled up as if in pain with his hands covering his face, his head bent forward until it almost touched his knees.

She watched him for a moment thinking he must be ill, and when he groaned again she felt she must do something to help him.

She moved to his side and stood there for a second or two thinking he might speak to her, but his face was still hidden.

At length she said gently and a little nervously:

"C . . can I . . . help you?"

She spoke, without thinking, in English, and the man was still. Then he answered, his voice muffled:

"No! There is nothing you can do!"

"But you are ill," Ancella insisted.

She thought he would reply, until he raised his head and she saw in consternation by the light of the Casino behind them that tears were running down his cheeks.

"I am not ill," he said in a voice that seemed dull with pain. "I am dead! Or at least I soon shall be!"

The memory of what she had read about suicides in Monte Carlo rushed into Ancella's mind.

"What do you . . . mean?" she asked.

"I mean what I say," he replied. "I have to kill myself – I have no alternative!"

Ancella's eyes widened, then she said quickly:

"You must not talk like that! It is wicked!"

"It is more wicked," he replied savagely, "to have killed my wife! For that is what I have done! I have killed her – do you hear?"

Ancella was stunned into silence, and as she looked at him apprehensively he said more quietly:

"I am sorry. You are a stranger and I should not burden you with this. But you asked me and I have told you the truth."

Ancella could see that he was an Englishman of about thirty-five, obviously a gentleman. At the same time she had never heard such suffering in a man's voice, and she had never seen a man cry before.

"Let me . . . help you," she asked softly.

There was a bitter twist to his lips as he replied:

"You are very kind, but there is nothing you can do. I have been a damned fool. It is what one expects here, is it not? That human beings should make fools of themselves!"

"Have you lost all your money?" Ancella asked sympathetically.

As she spoke she sat down beside the man on the bench, and he drew a handkerchief from his breast-pocket and wiped his eyes.

"I have lost everything that could have kept my wife living for at least a little longer."

He straightened himself and Ancella knew he was fighting for self-control as she asked:

"Is it really as bad as that?"

"It could not be worse!" he answered.

He gave the same bitter smile as he said:

"I suppose you are curious? It is to be expected. Well, I will tell you the truth. The Doctors have given my wife a month or two to live unless I can take her to Switzerland, to see a Specialist who operates on her unusual complaint with about a fifty-fifty chance of success."

He ceased speaking.

"And you were gambling to get the money for this particular operation?" Ancella asked.

"It is naturally very expensive," he replied, "and we had already sold everything we had, to come here, thinking the sunshine might work miracles."

He paused, then added violently:

"But God knows there were no miracles and now I have thrown away the last chance we had of being together."

He gave a deep sigh.

"I suppose really a month this side of eternity is not important."

"But of course it is!" Ancella said. "Is there nothing you can do?"

"Nothing," he answered, "except, I hope, die like a gentleman without making the fuss I was doing just now when you spoke to me."

"I did not want to embarrass you," Ancella said, "I thought you were ill."

"You have been very kind," the man replied, "and now I must go back to my wife and tell her what a mess I have made of everything. She will understand because she is that kind of person."

There was a warmth in his voice that had not been there before and Ancella suddenly saw the tragedy of what had happened.

They must have agreed, because they loved each other, to take the risk, to chance everything they possessed, knowing that if the money was lost there was nothing left but death for both of them.

The man rose to his feet.

"Thank you for listening to me."

He turned to walk away and suddenly Ancella made up her mind.

"Wait!" she said.

He already had his back to her and now he turned round and she could see he was very pale. Yet he was completely self-controlled and there was something almost heroic about it.

"What I am going to suggest to you may sound very strange," Ancella said, "but I want you to come back with me into the Casino and let me make one effort to help you."

"How could you do that?" he asked dully without much interest in his voice.

"Will you trust me?" Ancella asked.

"If you ask me to do so," he replied. "But I do not understand."

"Let me try what I have in mind without explanations," Ancella pleaded.

He looked at her and she felt that he saw her for the first time.

"Very well," he said quietly, "and let me thank you once again for being so sympathetic."

"I would like to be more practical than that," Ancella replied, "so trust me as you have promised to do."

She walked ahead of him back into the gambling rooms and he followed her.

She went to the table where she had played with the Princess.

She drew from her hand-bag 50 francs which she had left over from the money she had changed at Calais and changed them for one chip.

She stood looking at the Roulette wheel and as a chair was vacated by a woman playing at the table, a flunkey suggested she should sit in it but Ancella shook her head.

She wanted to stand exactly as she had stood when she had been placing bets for the Princess.

The Croupier spun the wheel and now as the white ball whirled round Ancella knew once again that number eleven would come up.

She put the chip into the hand of the man who stood beside her.

"Eleven!" she said.

As if he suddenly understood what she was trying to do, he bent forward and placed it on the table just as the Croupier said:

"Rien ne va plus."

The ball spun round twice again and Ancella held her breath.

"Onze, noir, impair et manque."

She turned to smile at the man beside her and saw him looking at her with a strange expression of incredulity in his eyes.

"How did you do that?" he asked.

"I cannot explain," Ancella answered.

The Croupier was taking the money from all the numbers except eleven, then he pushed 1750 francs onto number eleven and looked enquiringly at Ancella.

She was calculating exactly what she had gained. £70 would not, she thought, be enough for the operation or for a patient to stay for any length of time in an expensive clinic.

78

They also had to travel there and that would not be cheap.

The man beside her would have reached out towards the money, but she stopped him.

"Leave it!" she said.

"Are you wise?" he asked in a low voice and she knew how tense he was.

"Leave it!" Ancella repeated.

It seemed an interminable length of time before everyone had staked their bets.

Ancella knew while they waited that the man beside her thought she was crazy not to take the money they had gained from the table.

She was certain that had it been his francs they had staked he would have defied her and been content with what they had won rather than try for more.

"Well, at least," he said urgently, "let us put a few francs on *rouge ou noir*. It might be a saver."

Ancella shook her head.

"I asked you to trust me."

He took his eyes from the table and looked at her face.

"I think anyone would trust you," he said quietly.

She smiled at him but did not answer.

She heard the Croupier say:

"Rien ne va plus."

And a moment later the Roulette wheel was spinning.

Ancella was very still, and yet in some extraordinary way she was not apprehensive. She just knew with one of those strange convictions she could not explain to herself that the number eleven would turn up.

"Onze, noir, impair et manque."

As the Croupier said the words the man beside her gave a little sound that was indescribable.

"How can you have done it?" he asked.

"I have no idea!" Ancella answered, and it was the truth.

79

There was only one other person who had staked on eleven.

The Croupier pushed a great pile of winnings towards the number.

"Well over £2,000," Ancella calculated to herself.

It would be enough – she was sure it would be enough – for everything that was required to save the woman's life.

"Shall I pick it up now?" the man beside her asked in an unsteady voice.

"Yes."

Ancela signalled the Croupier, who pushed the money towards him and he threw some chips down onto the table for the employees and picking up the rest in both hands held it out towards Ancella.

"Will you take half?" he asked.

She shook her head.

"It is yours," she replied, "or rather your wife's. Now she can have her operation, and I have a feeling, just as strong as the feeling I had about winning, that it will be successful!"

She saw the tears come into his eyes. They had turned a little aside from the table and he said:

"I did not believe there was such kindness or such goodness left in the world."

He looked down at the money in his hands.

"Are you quite sure?" he asked unsteadily, "and what about your original stake?"

"Buy some flowers with it for your wife from me," she answered, "and tell her I shall be praying that you will both find happiness."

She turned and walked away from him as she spoke.

Because he was so moved by what she had said and bemused by what had happened, she was out of sight before he could find words in which to speak to her again.

Ancella found the Princess still talking to the Comte.

She did not join them but sat on a chair against the wall

where she could wait until she was wanted.

She suddenly felt strangely exhausted as if she had passed through an emotional experience.

Then she found herself praying that the money she had won would, of all the wins that were taking place in the Casino that night, really bring about good instead of evil.

Chapter Four

Dr. Groves arrived to visit the Princess the following morning, and having been with her for about a quarter-of-an-hour asked to speak to Ancella.

They moved downstairs into a Sitting-Room which was not as grand as the Salon but was still very attractive, with windows looking out towards Eza.

"The Princess speaks very highly of you, Miss Winton," Dr. Groves began.

"I am glad," Ancella replied. "I had hoped that I would justify Sir Felix's trust in me."

"I am sure you will do that."

Dr. Groves was not unlike Sir Felix Johnson in appearance, being about the same age and having the same charming manner.

Like Sir Felix he wore a conventional frock-coat and top-hat to visit his patients, and also a cravat expertly tied, in the centre of which was a tie-pin in the shape of a horse-shoe.

Everything in Monte Carlo, Ancella thought, was invariably an emblem of good luck.

"I will, however, be frank," Dr. Groves went on, "and say that I was expecting someone older. But as the Princess is satisfied, that is all that matters."

"Is Her Highness actually ill in any way?" Ancella asked.

She felt as she spoke that it was only a remote possibility, considering the late hours the Princess spent at the Casino and the fact that she apparently did everything she wished to do.

"I think, as you are acting in the capacity of Nurse to Her Highness," Dr. Groves said slowly, "you should know the facts about this particular case."

He paused, then asked with a faint smile:

"How old do you think the Princess is?"

It was a question Ancella had not expected.

"I have no idea," she answered, "but I should have thought from her appearance very old . . . well over seventy."

"As a matter of fact," Dr. Groves replied, "she is only sixty-two!"

Ancella looked surprised and he said:

"It is really a very sad story."

"Do tell me?" Ancella begged.

"The Princess was, I believe, very lovely when she was young," Dr. Groves began. "In fact when I first saw her some twenty years ago she was still outstandingly beautiful."

Recalling the Princess's profile Ancella could believe that was true, and she had in fact noticed last night when she was talking to Comte André that when she was excited and interested her face had a definite semblance of beauty.

"The Princess was married when she was quite young," Dr. Groves continued, "to Prince Serge Vsevolovski, a bridegroom chosen by her parents, who was fifteen years older than she was and, I should imagine, without exception the most outstandingly handsome man in Russia."

Ancella was just about to say:

"Then his son is like him," but she bit back the words.

"It was inevitable," Dr. Groves went on, "that the Princess should fall madly in love with her husband. He was very anxious to have children; the Princess, for no reason that I can ascertain, at first did not conceive a child, then later had several miscarriages. She was in fact thirty-five when Prince Vladimer was born."

"Prince Serge must have been very pleased," Ancella exclaimed.

"He was naturally delighted. Unfortunately this did not prevent his being consistently unfaithful."

Ancella looked at the Doctor enquiringly and he went on:

"One can quite understand the temptations. The Prince travelled a great deal, he visited England, was constantly in Paris, and of course when Monte Carlo became fashionable he came here."

He smiled.

"There were always extremely attractive women ready to throw themselves into his arms, and the Princess, who was very possessive, almost fanatically so, became more and more jealous."

Ancella's eyes were sympathetic as Dr. Groves continued:

"Having a child and the fact that she had been ill on and off for some years had taken a certain toll of her looks. She therefore consulted every beauty specialist known in Russia and in any other part of Europe. She tried 'quack' remedies of every sort and description."

Dr. Groves's voice sharpened as he went on:

"There are always charlatans who will make the most out of such a situation and batten on a rich woman, whatever damage they may inflict."

"What happened?" Ancella asked, already knowing the answer.

"One of these quacks," Dr. Groves replied, "sold her a 'miracle preparation' which he averred would change her appearance overnight to that of a girl of eighteen. You can see for yourself what occurred!"

"Her skin!" Ancella exclaimed.

"Exactly!" Dr. Groves agreed. "The so-called 'miracle preparation' destroyed the texture of her skin until it became as you see it now, criss-crossed with lines almost like a Chinese parchment."

This was exactly how Ancella had described it to herself, and now she felt a deep compassion for the Princess, who had sought to repair her beauty because she loved her husband.

"Can nothing be done?" she asked.

"Absolutely nothing!" Dr. Groves answered. "It has of course made Her Highness look immeasurably older, and while Prince Serge was alive it was an inexpressible tragedy. Now I do not think the Princess cares."

"I think every woman, however old she may be, cares about her appearance," Ancella replied.

"You are right of course," Dr. Groves conceded, "but the Princess has transferred her passionate, possessive love to her son. Whereas in the past she was jealous of her husband, she is now jealous of Prince Vladimer."

Ancella began to understand some of the things the Princess had said to her.

"I am telling you this," Dr. Groves went on, "as a warning, because at times the Princess may seem a little unbalanced, especially where her son is concerned."

"I had already guessed that in her mind she sometimes confuses him with her husband," Ancella said.

"That is very perceptive of you, Miss Winton," Dr. Groves exclaimed. "It is what I have imagined might be happening, but I have not been long enough with the Princess since she arrived here this year, to be certain."

"There is nothing we can do?" Ancella asked.

"Nothing!" Dr. Groves said. "Except keep her well, keep her from taking drugs of any sort, and keep her interested in other things besides Prince Vladimer and his love-affairs."

"Are there many of them?"

Ancella knew it was indiscreet but she could not help asking the question.

Dr. Groves shrugged his shoulders.

"In a place like this people only do two things," he answered. "They gamble and they gossip! If the latter is to be believed, wherever Prince Vladimer goes he leaves a mountain of broken hearts behind him."

The Doctor laughed.

"That may sound over-dramatic, Miss Winton, but I assure you I often have to treat broken hearts, although they are usually referred to by far more complicated medical terms."

Ancella had the feeling that, while he was talking impersonally, Dr. Groves was warning her.

She was certain this was the truth when he said slowly:

"If you find yourself in a difficulty of any sort, Miss Winton, I hope you will look on me as a friend with whom you may speak quite frankly. Sir Felix has told me how fond he was of your father, and I should like to feel that I was always there, should you need me."

"That is very kind of you, Dr. Groves, and I appreciate it," Ancella said. "I hope, however, not to be a nuisance in any way, but to look after the Princess as I came here to do."

She gave him a little smile and added:

"I was not expecting, however, to visit the Casino every night."

"When you have lived here as long as I have," Dr. Groves replied, "you will find it extremely boring, especially if you cannot afford to lose your money."

"I certainly cannot afford to do that!" Ancella exclaimed. "At the same time I find it very interesting to see the place which is looked on with such horror by many people in England."

"So I believe," Dr. Groves said, "and the Bishops have made violent attacks upon it. But quite frankly most of the accusations levelled are very exaggerated."

"I thought that must be the truth," Ancella replied, "except . . ."

She was about to mention the man last night who had gambled away everything he possessed; then she thought it would be a mistake to speak of it, even to Dr. Groves.

"The truth is the Casino receives too much publicity!" he exclaimed, "like 'The Man Who Broke the Bank at Monte Carlo'."

Ancella, who had heard the song, which had become a natural favourite and was played on every barrel-organ in London, laughed.

"Did he really exist?" she asked. "I thought he was just a fictitious character."

"No, indeed!" Dr. Groves replied. "His name was Charles Deville Wells, and I met him when he was here seven years ago."

"And he really did break the Bank?"

"Yes, indeed, he broke the Bank several times in three days. When that happens and the Roulette table runs out of money it is covered with a black crepe sheet until new boxes of gold and notes can be brought from the head office."

"How fascinating!" Ancella exclaimed. "And how much did Mr. Wells win?"

"It is always said," Dr. Groves answered, "that he turned his original capital of £400 into £40,000 in three days! He was an unpleasant little man, and he is now in prison!"

"In prison?" Ancella exclaimed.

"Too many people trusted him with their money! He obtained nearly £30,000 by inviting them to invest in his invention of a new type of fuel-saving device for coal-burning ships. Actually there was no invention!"

Ancella thought that there was certainly a case where money had not only brought no happiness to the winner, but had even made him a criminal.

Dr. Groves looked at his watch.

"I would like to stay here talking to you, Miss Winton," he said, "but I have half-a-dozen patients waiting for me, none of whom, I may add, are really in need of any urgent attention!"

He walked to the door, then paused.

"Look after the Princess," he said, "and yourself."

Again Ancella knew there was a warning in his voice, and when he had gone she went upstairs somewhat reflectively to find the Princess.

Her employer was in an extremely good humour, all due to the fact that the night before she had sat talking to Comte André until the early hours of the morning.

Going back in the carriage drawn by the four fast horses she had said to Ancella, with a new softness in her voice:

"Comte André de Valpré is a very dear friend of mine."

"I thought he must be," Ancella replied.

She was feeling sleepy. The hours had seemed very long while she sat waiting for the Princess to leave, but in a way it had been a relief that she did not have to stand at the Roulette table putting on her stakes.

"He was very kind to me when I was desperately unhappy," the Princess said.

She spoke as if she looked back into the past for her own satisfaction rather than Ancella's.

"I felt that my life was finished, but he showed me it could still hold a great deal of happiness and amusement."

"He fell . . . in love with you?" Ancella asked.

As soon as she spoke she felt she had perhaps been impertinent in making such a suggestion.

"But of course," the Princess answered. "And he was an ardent, an eloquent lover, as are most Frenchmen."

"Did you want to run away with him?" Ancella asked curiously.

The Princess laughed.

"There was no chance of that!" she answered. "He had a very jealous wife, as he still has. What is more, she holds the purse-strings!"

Then the Princess said with a note of venom that had not been there before:

"She is one of those title-hunting, multi-million-dollar American heiresses who descend on Europe like locusts, snatching up noblemen in the same manner as they snatch up pictures and *Objets d'art* of every description."

She obviously hated the Comte's wife so intensely that Ancella decided to ask no more questions, but the Princess was not so easily silenced.

"Women are harpies," she said. "*All* women! They want men for what they can get out of them. They suck them dry! They are insatiable – houses, horses, jewels, gowns – there is nothing they will not demand of a man, and of course if they are unscrupulous and clever enough they also force him to give them his name! I have warned Vladimer – I have warned him! But he does not listen to me any more than – Serge did."

Her voice dropped and she muttered almost beneath her breath:

"Harpies! Witches! Vampires without hearts, without souls, and men so foolish that they cannot escape them!"

There was silence as they journeyed on towards the Villa d'Azar. Then the Princess said more calmly:

"Mixed marriages between people of different nationalities are always a mistake."

She looked at Ancella and added:

"That English woman, the Marchioness – do you think she wants to marry my son?"

Ancella thought quickly, then replied:

"Your Highness forgets, I arrived only to-day."

"Yes – Yes, of course! But when Vladimer does marry – which need not be until I am dead – it must be to a Russian – a Russian!"

Ancella did not reply, but now as she went upstairs she thought that what Dr. Groves had told her about the Princess explained her outburst against women the night before.

She felt desperately sorry that in Her Highness's efforts to remain beautiful and attractive she had in fact destroyed everything she sought to preserve.

She understood now why the Princess rouged her face and reddened her lips, which was considered extremely improper in England. There it was only the unmentionable type of women who used cosmetics of any sort.

At least that was what her aunts had always told Ancella; but she could not help suspecting that the Marchioness's skin was not the pearly white it appeared to be in the evening, and that the wild-rose flush on her lips was not entirely due to nature.

But the Marchioness employed her aids to beauty very expertly.

Ancella had seen women in the Casino the night before who made no pretence about accentuating the natural colours of their faces in a most flamboyant manner, though there was no doubt it made some of them look exceedingly attractive.

The Princess was working on a new gambling system.

Her bed was covered with calculations on pieces of paper, with replicas of the Roulette board and half-a-dozen of the books which Ancella had learnt were on sale in Monte Carlo describing various 'infallible' systems.

There were dozens of them – the Turin Game, the Samur Game, the Triangle of Pascal, Dominating Numbers, The Differential Calculus as applied to Astrology.

They cost from 6d to £24 but Ancella was certain that if any of them were really successful the person who had invented them would not have felt obliged to write a book about it.

But she had seen quite a number of women in the Casino carrying one or other of them.

"I am considering that I might do better at Baccarat," the Princess said reflectively.

"I wonder if His Highness won last night," Ancella remarked without thinking.

"He was playing Baccarat?" the Princess asked.

"I think that was what he was going to do, after I had given him your message," Ancella replied.

"And who was with him?" the Princess enquired.

Too late Ancella realised it would have been better not to mention what had occurred, but there was now nothing for her to do but tell the truth.

"The Marchioness."

"She would be!" the Princess said sharply. "I am absolutely convinced that woman should not be staying here, and Boris tells me . . ."

She stopped as if she realised she had been about to be indiscreet and picking up one of the pieces of paper from her bed studied it.

It was soon time for the Princess to dress before luncheon, and when she was carried downstairs, with Ancella walking behind her, they went into the Salon to find the guests already assembled.

They were a party of twelve, with two distinguished couples from nearby Villas. Ancella was introduced to them but they made no effort to talk to her and she faded discreetly into the background.

At luncheon the conversation was general, which excused her from making any particular effort with the gentlemen on either side of her.

Prince Vladimer sat at the head of the table, with his mother at the opposite end.

Ancella noticed that the Princess appeared to be watching her son, noting every word he spoke to the Marchioness who, looking exceedingly beautiful, was on his right.

As the meal, which was delicious, drew to an end, the Princess asked:

"What are you doing this afternoon, Vladimer?"

"I am going to Monte Carlo, Mama."

He spoke to his mother with affection and warmth in his voice, and Ancella, who could not help looking at him during luncheon, thought again, as she had last night, that he was without exception the most attractive man she had ever seen.

It was not only that he was so handsome; it was also the animation in his face when he spoke, the twinkle in his grey-green eyes and the smile on his lips that she found somehow irresistible.

He had not spoken to her before the luncheon, for she had been at the other end of the room and almost as soon as the Princess had welcomed their guests the meal was announced.

Ancella thought, however, although she was not sure, that he glanced at her once or twice. Then she told herself she was conceited in thinking he was even aware of her existence.

"I wonder if it would be possible," the Marchioness said immediately after the Prince had spoken, "for me to have a carriage this afternoon? I have one or two purchases I must make in Beaulieu."

"But of course!" the Prince replied. "I will order the Victoria for you. You will find it most comfortable."

"Thank you, Vladimer," the Marchioness replied, smiling at him with an intimate look in her blue eyes which was very noticeable.

"If you are going to Beaulieu," Captain Sudley interposed, "I wonder if you would mind if I came too? I want to buy some new collar-studs, amongst other things."

"But of course!" the Marchioness answered, "as long as you do not mind my taking some time in the shops."

"I will try not to be impatient," he said with his loud laugh.

'He certainly arranged that cleverly!' Ancella thought to herself, remembering what she had heard him and the Marchioness plan when she had been hidden under the balustrade.

The other members of the house-party all appeared to have various things they wished to do, while Baron Mikhovovitch said quite firmly that he was going to lie down and rest.

"I find these late hours very tiring," he remarked.

"I find it even more tiring when one loses money!" someone laughed.

"That is true," the Baron agreed.

"Do you know, an extraordinary thing happened last night," Captain Sudley said.

"What was that?" the Marchioness enquired.

"I left you and His Highness playing at the Baccarat table," Freddie Sudley replied, "because I saw a man I know called Harnsworth. He is a member of my club as a matter of fact. He was standing by the Roulette table – the one you play at, Your Highness."

He turned to the Princess as he spoke, who was listening to him as was everyone else at the luncheon table.

"Harnsworth was standing there holding a considerable sum of money in both his hands," Captain Sudley continued. "I went up to him and said: 'Run of good luck, Harnsworth? I envy you!'

"He looked at me with an odd expression in his eyes. Then he answered: 'It was an angel who won it for me! Now she has disappeared and I cannot find her!'

" 'An angel?' I exclaimed. 'Good God! There are not many angels in this place!'

"I laughed as I spoke. As a matter of fact I thought he must have been drinking.

" 'It was an angel!' he persisted, 'and I cannot believe it!'

" 'I cannot believe it either!' I told him, 'but she seems

to have done you well! Are you going to have another flutter?'

"He did not answer for a moment then he said: 'I am going back to my wife, Sudley, and we are both going down on our knees to thank God for helping us!' "

Captain Sudley paused before he finished:

"He spoke in such a serious tone and with such conviction that I knew in fact that he was not only cold sober, but he also believed what he said!"

"What an extraordinary story!" the Baron exclaimed.

"I only wish an angel would help me!" the Marchioness cried and gave her light laugh which someone had once told her sounded like a peal of bells.

"Do you really believe him?" the Princess asked.

"Well, he must have had a hallucination of some sort," Captain Sudley replied. "At the same time it was a pretty substantial one, and I never knew Harnsworth have the sort of means that he could afford to gamble for high stakes."

"We must all go looking for angels!" the Marchioness exclaimed. "Would it not be lovely if we could find one?"

The Princess rose to her feet and luncheon was at an end.

Ancella was only too grateful that nothing more was said about an angel. They would soon forget about Mr. Harnsworth's win, she thought, when some other excitement happened in the Casino.

"Thank goodness no-one saw me with him," she told herself.

She was well aware that her life would be insupportable if the Princess and her guests thought there was any possible way in which she could bring them luck at the tables.

The Princess went to lie down and Ancella turned towards her own room.

This was her time off and she decided she would not

waste a moment of it by staying indoors, but would go into the garden.

She had the idea of making a sketch of the view towards Eza.

When her father had been ill and unable to leave his room she had often drawn sketches to amuse him.

Sometimes they were of people, sometimes they were of the countryside, the horses, the cows, a new haystack that had been erected, or perhaps the shrubs in the garden.

She had brought her sketch-pad with her to Monte Carlo and now taking up her pencils she thought that if the sketch looked attractive later she might colour it.

The sun was very warm and there was no wind as she went down the flight of marble steps into the garden.

The trees cast a cool shade and the flowers in their vivid colours were like jewels against their green background.

The sea was sparkling blue and to-day no waves were splashing against the promontory, but only very gently lapping.

Ancella did not walk to the balustrade. Instead she turned left and found a place she had noted before under the shade of a huge carob tree.

Here she had an almost perfect view of the Bay of Moors, and beyond it the summit of Eza threw its castle-like outline sharp and clear against the blue of the sky.

It was so lovely that for some minutes she could only sit looking at it until, almost as if she called herself to task for wasting time, she opened her pad and picked up her pencils.

She must have been drawing for some time, wondering as she did so if it would ever be possible to ask if she could have a carriage to drive to Eza or to the Peninsula of St. Hospice when the Marchioness and Captain Sudley were not there.

Then she told herself she was being very presumptuous:

of course she could not ask for a carriage, and if she wished to visit Eza she would have to do so on foot.

She wondered how long it would take her. Then, as she raised her head to look again at the high summit, she was aware that someone was standing just behind her.

Before he spoke she knew who it was.

"I did not know you were an artist," the Prince said.

Ancella would have risen to her feet, but he said quickly: "No, please do not move."

Ancella obeyed him and looked up as he towered above her, his head silhouetted against the dark green branches of a tree.

She met his eyes and somehow something strange happened, as it had last night in the Casino when she had first seen him.

They looked at each other and it was impossible to look away.

"So your name is correct!" he said.

She did not pretend to misunderstand.

"H .. how . . . did you know?" she asked nervously.

"Actually I saw you standing at the table with the man you helped," the Prince said.

"Your Highness . . . will not . . . tell the . . . others?"

"No, of course not," he answered. "I am only thankful for your sake that they did not see you, as I did."

She gave a little sigh of relief.

"There is so much I want to ask you," he said, "but we cannot talk here, you realise that?"

Almost involuntarily Ancella looked over her shoulder towards the Villa.

"Exactly!" he remarked. "For how long are you free?"

"Until five o'clock."

"I expected that. It gives us quite a long time."

Ancella waited.

She was not certain what he was about to suggest, but she knew she would agree, whatever it was.

"I am going back to the Villa," the Prince said. "I shall drive my car away as if I were going to Monte Carlo."

"Your . . . car?" Ancella questioned.

"Are you afraid to travel in one?"

"No, of course not!"

"Then I will wait for you a little way up the road. Turn right when you come out of the gate."

Ancella looked at him wide-eyed and he said with a smile:

"You are English. They will expect you to go for a walk."

Ancella did not speak and after a moment he said:

"Give me about ten minutes. The car does not always start as quickly as I should like."

He smiled again and then walked away casually.

As if he had just spoken to her in passing, he walked to the end of the small garden, then back again on the other side of it.

Ancella went on sketching, but she hardly knew what her pencil drew.

Her heart was beating quickly and a strange excitement was creeping over her.

The Prince wanted to talk to her and she wanted to talk to him.

It was something, she thought, that she should not do, and yet why not? He was her host. He was in a way her employer, as the Princess was.

He had told her to meet him and there was nothing wrong in that. Yet she knew that should their assignation become known it would not only seem peculiar, but it would also anger the Princess.

Dr. Groves had said she was fanatically jealous where Prince Vladimer was concerned.

Although it was ridiculous, Ancella told herself, to think that His Highness might be interested in any way in her, she was not so naive as to be unaware that the Princess would resent his taking an interest, however perfunctorily, in someone who was ostensibly her servant.

"I must be careful . . . very careful!"

She knew, however, although caution warned her not to go, that she had every intention of meeting the Prince as he had suggested.

She waited for ten minutes which seemed to pass very slowly. Then shutting her sketch-pad she walked slowly up the marble steps, across the terrace, through the Salon and up to her bed-room.

She put on one of the straw hats she had bought in London and which she had trimmed prettily with small white roses which complemented the white collar and cuffs which were attached to the pale lilac gown she wore.

Picking up her hand-bag and sun-shade she looked at herself in the mirror and realised that her eyes were shining with excitement.

"I must look casual," she told herself and deliberately walked slowly down the stairs into the hall.

When she reached the front door the Major Domo, who had been speaking to one of the footmen, came forward to say:

"If you wished to go to Beaulieu, *M'mselle*, Her Ladyship has already left."

"I am going for a walk," Ancella replied. "I must get some exercise."

The Major Domo smiled.

"*Ah! Les Anglaises!*" he exclaimed. "They always want their exercise! The French would rather rest at this time of the day!"

Ancella smiled at him and started to walk up the twisting drive, pausing to look at the geraniums so as not to appear to be in a hurry.

Only when she reached the gates which led onto the road and turned right, did she walk quickly with an eagerness she could not suppress, to find the Prince.

He was about a hundred yards down the road and when she saw his car she drew in her breath in surprise.

Painted bright yellow, it had a black hood which was open and red leather seats.

As she appeared the Prince came forward.

He held out his hand and when she gave him hers a little shyly he raised it to his lips.

"I was half-afraid you would not be brave enough to do as I suggested," he said.

"I wanted to see Your Highness's . . . car," Ancella murmured.

"And also, I hope, its owner!" he answered.

She looked at the car because she was too shy to look at him and he said:

"Let me help you in and I will drive slowly so as not to blow your hat away. At the same time, if you are nervous of losing it, I have a chiffon scarf which you can tie under your chin."

He handed her the scarf as he spoke and she could not help wondering how many women had used it before her.

He wound up the car which started easily, then jumped in beside her and drove off quite smoothly.

"What sort of car is it?" Ancella enquired.

"It is a Panhard," he answered, "and the very latest model. I bought one after the magnificent achievement of Émile Lebassor in the race from Versailles to Bordeaux three years ago."

"What did he do?" Ancella asked.

"Drove for forty-eight hours and forty-eight minutes. He only stopped once for a mere ten minutes at Bordeaux. It was a superhuman performance."

"But surely this is a new car," Ancella said.

"It is my third Panhard and has just been delivered," the Prince replied. "I ordered my second after the race from Paris to Marseilles. You must have heard about that!"

"I am afraid not!" Ancella said apologetically.

"What do you talk about in England?" the Prince asked and laughed. "Actually I thought everyone in the world must have heard of the race of over a thousand miles which was completed by no less than fifteen of the thirty-two cars which started."

"And the Panhard won?"

"It did indeed! And this new model can do fifteen miles an hour!"

As if he thought Ancella might be frightened at the thought, the Prince added:

"But I would not dare to take you as fast as that! I must remember you come from England, where until two years ago the speed limit was four miles an hour!"

"It has been altered now," Ancella said quickly.

"I know that," the Prince replied, "but you are fined if you exceed twelve miles an hour, which to my mind is ridiculous when in a very short time cars will be able to do thirty."

"That is too fast!" Ancella exclaimed.

"You cannot expect me to agree, as I have just joined the Automobile Club of Great Britain and Ireland," the Prince said. "It was formed last year."

"Do you intend to race in England?" Ancella asked.

She thought, as she spoke, it might ensure her being able to see him after she had left Monte Carlo.

"When you have races I shall try to win them!" the Prince answered. "In the meantime, there are plenty in France!"

As he was talking they were driving along the road, and now he turned off the Lower Corniche to start climbing up a narrow, twisting lane with deep gorges on one side of it, the hills rising on the other.

There were flowers nestling in the ravines and in the patches of grass clinging to the hill-side. Ancella could see crimson poppies, the pearly-white Stars of Bethlehem and wild orchids.

There were almond and nectarine trees covered with pink blossom, and the mimosa was a riot of gold.

It was so exciting to be conveyed in a car and to see the beauty all around her. At the same time Ancella found it difficult to think of anything but the Prince.

She was vividly conscious how attractive he was as he drove with an expertise which she recognised and admired.

Occasionally the road became rather bumpy and the Prince said:

"One day I will take you to Monte Carlo. To ensure that the spectators of the *Concours d'Élégance* are not enveloped in clouds of dust, Blanc has brought in an Italian expert who has covered the road-surface with tar."

"With tar?" Ancella questioned in surprise.

"It makes it smooth, delightful to drive on, and there is no dust," the Prince replied.

Ancella thought if that was true it would be a great improvement.

Although it seemed windy sitting in the front of the car, she knew they were leaving behind them a large cloud of dust which because of the heat, hung almost like a fog on the dry air.

Soon they reached the road above the Lower Corniche and now she could see the great rock of Eza and below it a few scattered houses surrounded by big, shady trees.

Beneath these some of the older inhabitants of the village were playing bowls, while small boys imitated them with marbles.

There was a large stone fountain and some of the peasant-women from the village were filling their vessels and washing their clothes.

Everyone stopped what they were doing as the car appeared and when the Prince drew it to a standstill under the shade of a large tree the villagers gathered round staring at it in awe and admiration.

The Prince chose from the others a boy of about fourteen and told him to be in charge of the car. Then helping Ancella to the ground he led the way to where she could see a narrow path leading up the rock.

"I hope you are feeling energetic," the Prince said. "It is an ascent of about five hundred feet."

"I like walking," Ancella replied.

"I had an idea you would," he said. "Do you live in the country?"

"Yes."

"I knew it! I was sure you were not a product of the town!"

She did not ask him how he knew and they walked on, climbing to where there was a large archway through which they entered the village itself.

There was a street too narrow for anything but a horse to climb, but it was well paved with an ornamental pattern of red bricks running through the centre.

The houses on either side had the quaint picturesqueness of a mediaeval town. They were solidly built and all the floors and doorways were arched with stone.

As they walked up the street Ancella had glimpses of queer old staircases, of stone statues, behind small wrought-iron gates, and creepers falling in colourful profusion over the walls.

There were rhododendrons, azaleas, roses and sweet-scented honeysuckle, but still the Prince led her on until they reached the end of the village and the very summit of Eza itself.

Here there were some rough stone walls that might once have belonged to Saracen times and against them there was a seat surrounded by flowers overlooking the sea.

It was shaded by a canopy of wild roses and convolvulus,

and as Ancella sat down she thought she could not imagine a more romantic spot or a more breath-taking view.

They could see the coast-line for miles on either side and in front of them the Mediterranean, deep blue, shading to vivid emerald, shimmering in the heat of the afternoon sun.

"It is lovely!" Ancella exclaimed as the Prince sat down beside her. "Thank you for bringing me to a place that is so beautiful!"

"As I said, I wanted to talk to you," the Prince said, "and at least here we are alone where no-one will see us."

Ancella did not reply. She was looking at the view, and yet while she did so she was conscious that the Prince's eyes were on her.

"I am not surprised," he said quietly, "that the man in the Casino took you for an angel. I thought you looked like one the moment I saw you!"

There was a note in his voice that made Ancella look at him quickly. Then her eyes dropped so that her lashes were very dark against her pale cheeks.

"I . . . I think perhaps he . . . exaggerated something that was . . . just a . . . lucky chance."

"Was it really that?" the Prince asked.

Because she felt she must answer him truthfully Ancella said:

"He was desperate. He had gambled away everything he had, hoping to pay for an operation his wife needed. As they had nothing left, they would both have died if I had not been able to help them."

"How were you able to do that?"

"I . . . I was just . . . convinced that a certain number would . . . come up."

"How did you know it?"

"I cannot . . . explain."

Ancella made a little helpless gesture with her hands as she spoke.

"And do you think you could help everyone in the same way?"

"No. I am sure it would be impossible," Ancella answered quickly. "As I have said, it was just . . . chance, and he was in despair! If it was money wanted only for . . . pleasure, then I am sure it would be . . . impossible for me to do anything."

She paused to add:

"That is why I . . . beg you not to . . ."

The Prince put out his hand and laid it on hers.

"You do not have to say that to me," he said. "I knew at luncheon exactly what you were feeling."

"You . . . knew?" Ancella asked.

It was hard to speak because the touch of his hand had given her a very strange sensation.

She could not explain it to herself. It was as if the excitement which she had felt ever since he had asked her to meet him had intensified until it was almost a pain, and yet at the same time – wonderful!

"Ancella, look at me!" the Prince said in his deep voice.

It did not surprise her that he had used her Christian name.

Obediently she turned her head and raised her eyes to his.

"You are very beautiful!" he said, "but that is not important."

His grey-green eyes looked into hers and he went on:

"I know it is too soon to explain, too soon for words, and yet I think you are aware, as I was, that something happened when we met each other last night."

Ancella found it impossible to speak, and yet she felt as if just by looking at each other they were saying so much that could not be put into words.

The Prince gave a little sigh and took his hand from hers.

"I am rushing you – it is too soon and I should have waited," he said. "I know all the arguments, but somehow

104

they have no substance, no reality. It is what I feel at this moment that matters and I have the idea, although I may be wrong, that you understand."

Still Ancella could not answer him and after a moment he said:

"You are so lovely – so unbelievably beautiful, as so many men must have told you."

Now Ancella managed a little smile.

"No . . . one has said . . . that."

"I am the first?"

She nodded her head.

"And you have never been kissed?"

Now the colour rose in her cheeks as she said firmly:

"Of course . . . not!"

"Oh, my dear, I did not believe it was possible to find a woman who looked like you, to meet her in the Casino, and know that she was unspoilt, untouched and an angel!"

He smiled as he added:

"Perhaps it was prophetic that you were called Ancella when you were born."

"Few people know it is a derivative of the Greek for . . . 'angel'."

"My Greek is somewhat rusty," the Prince answered, "but I knew that as soon as you introduced yourself."

"You should not be . . . talking to me like . . . this," Ancella said with an effort. "I am employed by Her Highness, and if she knew that we were . . . together . . . I think she would send me . . . back to England."

"That is why, my sweet angel, we must be very careful," the Prince said.

Ancella drew herself up.

"There will be nothing to be careful about, Your Highness."

He gave a little laugh.

"Now you are rebuking me and quite rightly! At the

same time we have jumped so many fences already, you and I, that we cannot go back to the starting point. It is impossible!"

Ancella thought it was impossible, too, but she told herself severely that she must not allow the Prince to speak so intimately.

"You brought me here to see Eza . . ." she began.

"I did nothing of the sort," he interrupted. "I brought you here because I had to talk to you and to see you alone. You have not been at the Villa long, but you must know that Boris reports to my mother everything that occurs. He listens at doors, and what he does not hear – he invents!"

"I thought that," Ancella said, and she knew now who had examined her room when she had first arrived. "But if you know it . . . why do you . . . keep him?"

"Because he has always been my mother's personal servant and she likes to know everything that goes on. It amuses her and as a general rule it hurts no-one else. At the same time . . ."

His expression darkened as he said in a different tone:

"I distrust Boris and I have never liked him."

"I think he is a horrible man!" Ancella said. "And I am afraid of him!"

"He has not been impertinent to you?" the Prince asked sharply.

"No, no, of course not! It is just that he is . . . creepy and it is very un-English to feel that one is being . . . watched."

She thought of telling the Prince she was sure Boris had examined her room and her possessions, but she knew that she had no proof and it would sound rather petty.

"I want my mother to be happy," the Prince said. "As the Doctor will have told you, at times she gets very distressed and upset. So when she stays with me here or anywhere else I try not to upset her. That is why I do not wish her to know that we met this afternoon. And not for any other reason!"

He spoke emphatically and sincerely, and Ancella knew that he was telling her that he was not ashamed of his desire to see her and would, if he had his way, be quite open about it.

She felt pleased. At the same time she could not help wondering what the Marchioness would think.

"Tell me about yourself," the Prince pleaded.

"There is very little to tell," Ancella answered.

"Since my mother died I have lived quietly in the country. For the last year I have been nursing my father who was very ill and died only last month."

"So that you have had very little social life and met very few men."

"Very few," she said with a smile.

"Perhaps that is why you are so unspoilt, and so unique!" the Prince said. "At the same time, there is something more."

"What is that?" she asked without thinking.

"The feeling you and I have for each other."

"Perhaps you are . . . mistaken about . . . that," Ancella said. "It may be just because we met . . . unexpectedly . . . and later you saw me doing . . . something which may not occur again in a . . . thousand years."

"And if it does – I shall be there!" the Prince exclaimed. "Just as I am sure that a thousand years ago we may have sat in this very place and talked or found each other as we did last night."

There was a note in his voice that made her vibrate in a manner that she could not explain.

When she had heard him talking on the balustrade it had been his voice she had found herself listening to rather than the words he spoke.

Now it was almost like music and something within her responded to it, so that it was hard not to put out her hand to touch him.

107

"You will say that because I am Russian my emotions are more easily aroused than if I were European. But I swear to you, Ancella, that I have never in all my life felt like this about a woman!"

"What are you . . . trying to . . . say to . . . me?" Ancella asked in a whisper.

"I am saying that the moment I saw you I fell in love!"

"But that is . . . absurd!"

"Is it?" he asked. "Did you not feel as I did when we looked at each other? We both knew that something strange had happened, that we recognised each other."

"It . . . cannot be . . . true!" Ancella said shakily.

"It is true – and you know it!" he replied. "When I brought you here to-day I did not intend to say this or anything like it. I wanted to talk to you, perhaps to charm you or, perhaps more truthfully, to woo you. Instead I have said all that I am feeling in my heart. I want you to answer me from your heart."

"It is . . . impossible! You know it is . . . impossible!"

Even as Ancella spoke she remembered that Russian marriages were arranged, just as they were in France and often in England.

She remembered what the Princess had said about 'mixed marriages', and she knew that, if the Prince was talking of love, it was not the love that ended in marriage.

With a superhuman effort she forced herself to say stiffly:

"I think Your Highness is making a mistake, and because, as I am employed by your mother, it is essential for me to be absolutely circumspect, I must not listen to you. Either we must talk of other things or we must return to the Villa."

"I knew you would think it too soon," the Prince said. "But it is impossible when I am with you to do anything but speak the truth, feeling that any subterfuge or pretence between us is unnatural."

He sighed.

"I can only ask you to forgive me."

He held out his hand palm upwards.

"Do you forgive me, my little Greek angel?"

Ancella felt herself quiver at the passion in his words. Then because she could not help herself she laid her hand in his.

His fingers tightened, then he kissed her hand and she felt her whole body become weak at the touch of his lips.

He released her and rising to his feet said:

"Come! I must take you back, but first we will drink a glass of wine in the Tavern which is very old and was, I am sure, here when the Romans came."

Slipping a little on the smooth stones, they walked a short distance down until the Prince opened the door of a house which had the sign of a Ram outside it.

Inside it was very dark and cool.

There was an oak bar at one end and there were two wooden settles with heavy wooden tables in front of them.

They sat down on one and the Prince ordered a bottle of wine from an attractive woman dressed in peasant-costume with a white embroidered linen apron.

As she was getting it, there was the cry of a baby wailing fitfully in a back room, and when she came back with the bottle Ancella said in French:

"Is that your baby crying, *Madame*?"

"He is teething!" the woman replied, "and he is so fretful that I can do nothing with him. He cries not only all day, but also at night and it makes my husband very angry. Pray excuse, *Madame*, if he annoys you."

She went away before Ancella could speak, to come back with a plate of olives and carrying the baby under one arm.

He was a small, dark, rather undersized baby, and he looked unhappy as if he too had passed a number of sleepless nights.

"Have you tried giving him honey?" Ancella enquired.

"*Miel?*" the woman exclaimed. "Why?"

"It will soothe him and make him sleep," Ancella explained.

"There is plenty of honey round here," the woman said. "How much shall I give him?"

"Just give him a little on the tip of your finger," Ancella suggested, "and put half a teaspoonful in his bottle."

Thinking the woman was looking at her suspiciously, she tried to reassure her.

"I promise you it will keep him from crying, and it will also make him grow strong. Honey is very good for babies."

"I've never heard of that!" the woman exclaimed. "But now I think of it, my mother-in-law sometimes rubs it on an aching tooth."

She went to the bar, looked around, found what she was seeking and put the pot of honey on the counter.

Ancella rose to her feet.

"Let me hold the baby while you give it to him," she suggested.

The woman looked at her in surprise and put the baby in her arms.

He was still whimpering fitfully.

Ancella held him close against her and rocked him gently. He gave one small, feeble cry, then he was silent.

Having opened the pot the woman found a spoon and dug out a little honey and transferred it to the tip of her finger.

She paused to say:

"You are quite certain it will not hurt him?"

"I promise you will be surprised what a difference it will make," Ancella replied.

The mother put the honey into the baby's mouth. He opened his lips as if to cry, then started to suck avidly.

110

"He likes it!" she said in surprise. "Shall I give him some more?"

"Just a little, but not too much!" Ancella answered. "Later he will be thirsty, so he will want a drink; but you can give him some honey whenever he feels fretful. It will not hurt him, and always give it to him last thing at night. It will help him to sleep."

"Well, I never!" the woman exclaimed. "You sound as though you have half-a-dozen of your own."

"I hope one day I will have a son," Ancella replied with a smile.

The woman gave the baby a little more honey which he sucked appreciatively. Then as Ancella held him in her arms he closed his eyes as if satisfied.

"I really believe he is going to sleep!" the mother exclaimed in surprise.

"Put him into his cot and tuck him up warmly," Ancella said. "He will sleep, and when he wakes for his feed give him a little honey after it, and do not forget it last thing at night when you want to go to sleep."

"I'll remember," the woman said, "and not only will I bless you, *Madame*, but so will my husband! He is fed up with being kept awake!"

"I am sure he is," Ancella said. "You might try giving him some honey as well!"

The woman laughed as if she thought it was a joke. Then she said:

"You *mean* that, Madame?"

"I do mean it," Ancella said. "It makes everyone sleep well, especially babies and old people."

"*Tiens*, we certainly live and learn!" the woman remarked as she took the baby away.

Ancella felt she had neglected the Prince and she smiled at him a little shyly as she sat down with him again on the wooden settle.

"Is a ministering angel never off duty?" he asked.

She knew he was teasing her and she smiled as she said:

"My father found honey the one thing that made him sleep, and I was always quite sure it made him better-tempered!"

"You are full of surprises!" the Prince said. "As that woman so rightly remarked, one lives and learns!"

Ancella sipped her wine. It had a delicate flavour and although it was not such an exceptional wine as those they drank at the Villa, she enjoyed it.

The Prince was watching her and the fact that his eyes were on her face made her feel shy.

"This place is very old," she said, looking round the dim, low ceilinged Tavern. "I wonder how many people through the ages have sat here and worried about themselves and their future."

"I am not concerned with the past or the future," the Prince rejoined, "just the present and – you."

She felt herself quiver at the passionate note in his deep voice. He went on:

"You know that what has happened to us is different from what has ever happened before in our lives!"

"In my . . . life," Ancella agreed, "but . . ."

"There are no 'buts' where we are concerned," he interposed. "This is quite different and very wonderful."

Ancella met his eyes and drew in her breath.

Somewhere far away she heard a clock strike.

"We should go . . . back," she said.

"It is impossible to believe that time can go so swiftly," the Prince answered.

He put down his glass, laid several francs beside it, and rose to his feet. As he opened the door he called:

"Au revoir, Madame, et merci!"

"Merci beaucoup, Monsieur et Madame! You have been very kind. Please come again soon."

"We will do that," the Prince promised.

They went out into the hot sunshine and started to walk downhill to where the car was waiting for them, still surrounded by a crowd of admiring peasants.

The Prince helped Ancella into the front seat and over-tipped the small boy who had looked after it. Then, having started up the engine he drove off.

It was rather a hair-raising descent down the twisting road and Ancella recalled stories of cars whose brakes had failed and caused accidents.

But there were no mishaps and just as they reached the end of the road where it joined the Lower Corniche the Prince asked:

"You have been happy with me?"

"You . . . know I have!" Ancella replied.

"That is all I wanted to hear," he said. "Somehow we must contrive to be together again, to-morrow or the next day, but it may not always be easy. You do understand?"

"I understand," Ancella said a little stiffly.

"I know what you are thinking," the Prince said, "and it is not true. I want to be with you. I want to take you everywhere, to show you the world, but just for the moment it is impossible."

He paused and then went on slowly:

"I am not going to explain because I believe there is no need for words between us. All I ask is for you to trust me. Will you do that?"

He spoke with such a note of sincerity in his voice that Ancella knew she would have done anything and promised anything he might have asked of her.

She looked up at him and their eyes met. The world stood still.

"I do . . . trust you," she whispered.

Chapter Five

"We must go back."

"There is no hurry."

"What will the servants think?"

The Marchioness sat up as she spoke, making a little sound of pain as if her back was stiff.

"Damn the servants!" Freddie Sudley ejaculated. "This is the first time I have enjoyed myself since we came South!"

"I feel guilty," the Marchioness said, "not because we are here, but because we should be concerning ourselves with worrying as to how we can pay our bills. I had a poisonous letter from Paquin this morning."

"How poisonous?"

"They are threatening to sue me!"

"How much do you owe them?"

"Nearly two thousand pounds!"

"Good God, Lily!" Freddie Sudley exclaimed. "How can you have spent so much money?"

"I have to have clothes," the Marchioness said. "As you well know, it is only men who think that one is beautiful unadorned and talk about 'not painting the lily'!"

"But surely the paint need not be so exorbitantly expensive?"

"I imagined when I ordered most of the gowns that Lord Corwen was going to pay for them, but as you know he sheered off and married that young pudding-faced girl simply because her father's estates march with his."

"Corwen behaved disgracefully, as we well know,"

Freddie Sudley said, "and that is why the Prince . . ."

"I know – I know," the Marchioness interrupted. "There is no need to say it over and over again, but I shall have to do something soon."

"What sort of thing?" Freddie Sudley enquired.

He had been looking up at the branches of the tree above him and now he too sat up and tightened his tie.

"I really do not know," the Marchioness said. "I lay awake last night after we came back from the Casino and wondered what I could be doing wrong."

"I thought the Prince seemed pretty 'gone' on you at the beginning of the evening," Freddie Sudley said.

"He was," the Marchioness agreed, "when we met him after he had been to dinner with the Grand Duke Mikhail he seemed really pleased to see me."

She gave a little sigh.

"Then when we went to play Baccarat," she went on, "I suggested that I should sit beside him, but he wanted me to play too. He gave me some money, but you know as well as I do it is impossible to be intimate when one is playing at the tables."

"Did you win?" Freddie Sudley asked with a different note in his voice.

"A little," the Marchioness replied. "Which meant I could keep everything the Prince gave me. I have brought it for you. You will find it in my bag."

"Thank you, Lily!"

Captain Sudley reached out as he spoke and picked up the Marchioness's pale-blue satin bag from where she had put it at the foot of a tree.

He opened it and gave a low whistle.

"Quite a haul!"

"Send some of it to your creditors in England," the Marchioness begged. "Promise me, Freddie, you will do that?"

"We will stop at the Post Office on the way back,"

Freddie Sudley answered. "Even £100 will make them feel things are moving in the right direction."

"£100 will not go very far where Paquin is concerned!"

There was silence, then the Marchioness said:

"I have an idea!"

"What is it?" Freddie Sudley asked.

"I have tried almost everything on the Prince," she answered. "I have been provocative, I have been inviting, I have been cool, I have been aloof. I have even tried making him jealous."

"With any result?"

"He has been charming, flattering, considerate, but he has never said what I wanted him to say."

"What is your idea?" Freddie Sudley prompted.

"Do you remember how Daisy Warwick captured the Prince of Wales?"

"His Royal Highness was certainly caught hook, line and sinker, but I was never certain how she landed her fish."

"I will tell you," the Marchioness said. "She cried on his shoulder and asked his help."

"What for?" Freddie Sudley enquired.

"You must remember, or perhaps you were abroad with your Regiment," the Marchioness replied. "It was all over a very indiscreet letter she wrote to Lord Charles Beresford. Lady Charles opened it and threatened to publish! The Prince of Wales tried to help Daisy but failed."

"And while the negotiations were taking place His Royal Highness fell in love?" Freddie Sudley enquired.

"Exactly! And the only thing I have not tried on the Prince are tears!"

"Most men dislike women who cry," Freddie Sudley remarked.

"You care when I cry."

"Of course I do, but you are different."

"The Prince also must think I am different," the Marchioness said. "I will cry on his shoulder and I will look very alluring, and very – inviting while I do so."

Freddie Sudley made an exaggerated sound.

"Keep what you do to yourself!" he said harshly. "You know I cannot bear to think of you with another man, even while there is no alternative."

"No, there is no alternative," the Marchioness agreed. "But, Freddie, you know whom I love?"

He turned towards her.

"Do you really love me?" he asked. "More than any other man you have ever known?"

"You know I do," the Marchioness said with a note of sincerity in her voice. "Oh, Freddie, if only you were rich! How happy we would be and what fun we could have together!"

"If wishes were horses, beggars could ride."

"And we are beggars," the Marchioness sighed, "hopelessly in debt, both of us in danger of being taken to Court and without an idea of a solution!"

"I thought you had just come up with one."

"It is certainly worth a try," the Marchioness said reflectively, "in fact the more I think about it, the more I am sure it will succeed. There is nothing more appealing to a strong, masterful man than a weak and helpless woman."

"Let us hope you are right."

"I hope so too," she said, "and we must take no more risks. It was really crazy to come here like this, this afternoon."

"I do not see why," Freddie Sudley said sullenly. "We said we were going to look at the view, and God knows that is about the only thing that is free in this part of the world!"

The Marchioness reached out and picked up her bag

from where he had put it beside her. She drew out a small mirror, looked at her reflection and gave an exclamation of horror.

"I look a mess! My hair is falling down at the back and I am sure the maid at the Villa will think it strange how creased my gown is."

"Put your hat on," Freddie said, "and you will look stunning, as you always do. When you stand up I will brush you down."

"Men are so lucky!" the Marchioness said peevishly. "Whatever you do it never seems to make any difference to your appearance."

Freddie smiled.

"I would not care if it did! It has been wonderful to be alone with you here this afternoon, Lily. I was beginning to think I should go crazy if I had to go on making polite chit-chat, never having you to myself, even for a second."

"That ghastly servant, Boris, is everywhere!" the Marchioness said. "He looks at me with those hooded eyes of his and I feel that at any moment I shall find myself hysterically confessing my sins simply because I am frightened of him."

"The Russians are masters of interrogation," Freddie answered. "If he is being impertinent, I should tell the Prince. After all, he is Her Highness's servant – not his."

"You know Vladimer would not hear a word against his mother," the Marchioness said crossly. "I said something the teeniest bit critical about her the other day and he snapped my head off."

"That was a stupid thing to do," Freddie remarked.

"I know. I will not do it again."

The Marchioness put on her head her large straw hat, trimmed with blue and white flowers to match her gown, and skewered it into place with two long blue-topped hat-pins.

She smiled beguilingly at the man beside her.

"I suppose we must go," she said and realised that Freddie Sudley was looking at her with a touch of fire in his eyes.

"If you look at me like that," he said, "I will not be able to let you."

"Oh, please, Freddie, do not get excited all over again," the Marchioness exclaimed quickly. "We have been away for hours as it is. The servants will come to look for us if we are not careful."

"The servants! You are always worrying about the servants!" Freddie said angrily. "It is my feelings you should be considering."

"It is your predicament and mine which I *am* considering," the Marchioness replied with a touch of dignity. "I am trying to get us out of the appalling mess in which we find ourselves, and for Vladimer to have the slightest suspicion that we were more than friends would, as you know, ruin everything!"

She spoke so gravely that Freddie Sudley capitulated.

"You are right. We must go back."

He rose to his feet and putting out his hands helped the Marchioness to hers. Then he put his arms around her and kissed her gently on the lips.

"Thank you, my darling. You have been marvellous this afternoon, but then you always are!"

The Marchioness disengaged herself and started to shake out her skirts.

"Brush me down at the back, Freddie, and there are some dried leaves on your trousers."

They inspected each other carefully. Then, picking up her blue sun-shade, the Marchioness strolled ahead of him through the trees until they came in sight of the Victoria with its liveried servants waiting at the road-side.

The footman helped them in and the Marchioness said:

"Return to the Villa, but stop first at the Post Office in Beaulieu."

"Certainement, Madame," the footman said, then climbed onto the box beside the coachman.

The Marchioness opened her sunshade and held it elegantly over her head.

She was thinking as they drove along the narrow, dusty road of St. Hospice how pleasant it would be to own Victorias, Broughams, Cabriolets, Landaus and the servants to drive them, always ready at her command.

* * *

Ancella went to the Princess's bed-room punctually at five o'clock only to find that her services were not required.

"She's got that gypsy woman with her, *M'mselle*," Maria told her, "and the astrologer coming later. *Le Bon Dieu* knows they're not worth the time and money Her Highness wastes on them, but it amuses her."

"Shall I go to my room?" Ancella asked. "And if Her Highness needs me, perhaps you would let me know."

"You do that, *M'mselle*," Maria agreed, "and have a little rest. I hear you've been out walking. It's too tiring for you in this heat."

Ancella realised the fact that she had been out for a walk had already been discussed in the Villa, doubtless by most of the staff.

She felt a little throb of fear in case they should know where she had really been, but she told herself that the Prince had been exceedingly careful.

When he had left her a little way from the Villa he had driven off to Monte Carlo, and it was very unlikely that anyone would realise that he was arriving there two hours later than he would have done if he had gone there directly after luncheon.

She walked back to the Villa feeling dazed, and the sunshine seemed more golden than it had before.

It was impossible not to think over and over again of what the Prince had said to her, to think of his lips on her hand, almost to feel the touch of them still lingering on her skin.

In her own room she stood looking out at the blue of the sea and thinking everything had a new magic that had not been there before.

How could she ever have guessed or even imagined there was a man somewhere in the world like Prince Vladimer who would say such enchanting things and would arouse sensations within herself she had never known existed.

"Is this love?" she asked and was afraid of the answer.

It was all too perplexing, too difficult to understand. What did he mean by saying he had fallen in love with her? and if he had, what did he intend?

He had said he was not concerned with the future but with the present. But Ancella, unsophisticated though she was, knew that was a dangerous creed.

In the future he could go back to Russia, leaving, as Dr. Groves had warned her, a mountain of broken hearts behind him. But for her there was only England and the restricted, narrow existence of living with her aunts, unless . . .

Ancella's mind shied away from the alternative.

She told herself it was crazy to imagine for one moment that Prince Vladimer would wish to marry an unknown Englishwoman who was Nurse-Companion to his mother.

Even if he was prepared to contemplate a 'mixed marriage', such as the Princess had spoken of so scathingly, it would certainly not be with someone whom he thought of as his Social inferior.

In those circumstances how could she trust even for one moment his protestations of love?

It was all so depressing, and yet at the same time she could not help feeling an inexpressible elation and happiness just because of the things he had said and the way he had looked at her.

No man, she thought, should be so handsome, so irresistibly attractive! It was not fair on women!

She sat at the window looking out for so long and thinking of the Prince, that she suddenly realised with a start that it was time she began to dress for dinner.

The lady guests of importance like the Marchioness had their baths brought by the maids to their bed-rooms. Great silver cans containing hot and cold water were carried in and emptied into a hip bath which was arranged in a convenient place on the carpet.

Ancella knew they were arranged the same way in the great houses of England, and any lady of importance would be horrified at the idea of appearing in the passages wearing a dressing-gown.

But the Villa contained, to Ancella's surprise, several bath-rooms, and there was one almost adjacent to her bed-room which she was told she could use.

It was lavishly decorated with a white marble floor, tiled walls and ornate gold taps, and she thought privately that it was an improvement on the inconvenience of having to keep filling up the bath that was brought to one's bed-room with either hot or cold water.

In the bath-room she could lie stretched out in the warm water, and she wondered why more people did not have a bath-room attached to their bed-room, which would save, apart from anything else, an immense amount of labour.

Not that that was important in rich houses where there were innumerable men and women servants to carry the silver or brass cans for any distance and up many flights of stairs.

Ancella scented her bath with oil of violets which came, she saw on the bottle, from Grasse.

She wondered if she would ever have a chance of seeing the factory which she knew supplied all the famous French perfumes.

"There are so many things I would like to do if I had

122

the time," she told herself, and wondered how long she would be able to stay on the Cote d'Azur.

When she went back to her bed-room she went to the wardrobe to take out her evening gown and realised that while she had been bathing the maid had come into the room and laid her evening things out on the bed.

There were two gowns lying side by side, the white one which she had bought before leaving London and the black she had brought with her, thinking she might wear it if perhaps she and the Princess were alone in the evenings.

Now Ancella eyed it speculatively and thought that perhaps it was the gown she should wear to-night.

She had been vividly conscious of the danger of some-one connecting her with Mr. Harnsworth's win which Captain Sudley had described so graphically at luncheon.

"Perhaps if they saw me in white again," Ancella told herself, "they would remember seeing me last night."

It was an outside chance, and yet the risk was there.

"I will wear the black gown," she told herself and wondered if the Prince disliked black and if in consequence he would not think her beautiful.

Despairingly she told herself she must not keep thinking of the Prince: what he thought or did not think should not influence her in doing what was sensible.

At the same time, when she was dressed she looked at her reflection in the long mirror which stood in a mahogany frame in one corner of the room and thought perhaps she looked quite drab and insignificant.

As it happened, she looked neither of these things.

The black gown was made of a very light material and trimmed round the shoulders with spotted net. It was not a heavy black and Ancella had used her unerring good taste when she bought it.

It was a young girl's gown and did not in fact make her look any more sophisticated than did the white gown.

But what Ancella did not realise, because she was looking at the gown rather than herself, was that it was a perfect frame for her white skin.

It seemed to accentuate the fragile etherealness of her small pointed face, her large grey eyes and the soft, very pale gold of her hair.

She was without jewellery, and yet ornamented with a beauty which was somehow spiritual.

As she walked into the Salon behind his mother, the Prince thought that she looked like the first pale fingers of the sun when rising over the horizon they seem to push away the sable of the night which still covers the sky.

Then hastily he looked away because he was afraid that the expression on his face might be too revealing.

To-night there were over twenty-four people for dinner: the table was decorated with orchids and lit by enormous gold candelabra which the Princess had brought with her from Russia.

The dinner was even more superb than it had been the night before: there were too many courses as far as Ancella was concerned, although she had grown wise and ate very sparingly of those that came first so that she would not have to refuse dish after dish as the meal progressed.

To-night among the guests there were several extremely gay and amusing French people, and as there was no stiffness at the Villa parties, everyone talked across the table and did not confine themselves to their partners on either side.

Ancella found herself amused and interested just by listening to what was being said.

There were discussions in politics, gossip about many of the people staying in Monte Carlo, and of course about the Prince of Wales who was at Cannes.

Only the Princess seemed a little pensive. Ancella wondered whether the astrologer or the gypsy had given her discouraging predictions, then she told herself that it was unlikely.

They were too clever not to give their clients hope, if nothing else, and if the Princess was quiet it might be because she was tired, or perhaps she was wanting the dinner to pass quickly so that she could meet Comte André at the Casino again.

It was impossible for Ancella not to glance occasionally towards the end of the table, although she tried not to do so.

When she looked at Prince Vladimer, so handsome, and so at ease, laughing and talking either to the Marchioness on his right or a vivacious French Comtesse on his left she wondered if she had dreamt what had happened this afternoon and all he had said to her.

Had she been mistaken? Had she misunderstood the words he had spoken and the look in his eyes?

Compared with the women around the table Ancella felt very young and very unsophisticated.

"What do I know of life or . . . love?" she asked herself.

She was only a young girl from the country, ignorant of the social world, not even having 'come out' as a débutante, as she would have done had her mother been alive.

Quite suddenly she wanted to run away, she wanted to go back to England to be alone, and she knew that the reason was the pain she felt within her when she looked at the Prince.

A pain which lay in her heart.

Immediately dinner was finished the Princess was in a hurry to get to Monte Carlo.

She bustled the ladies into the Salon, then was carried upstairs to her own bed-room, instructing Ancella as she did so to fetch her evening-cloak as she had no intention of waiting for anyone.

As had happened the night before, the other guests lingered behind and Ancella found herself alone with the Princess, driving at what seemed break-neck speed along the road towards Monte Carlo.

125

"I am going to play Baccarat to-night," the Princess announced.

"I hope you win, Ma'am," Ancella replied.

"My astrologer tells me that my stars are right. Admittedly he could not pin-point the actual day that they are all in my favour, but it will certainly be one evening this week."

"I shall be interested to watch you," Ancella said. "It looks a little difficult to understand."

"The only difficulty," the Princess retorted, "is drawing the winning card."

That was irrefutable. Ancella lapsed into silence and looked out of the window, wondering whether the baby in the tavern was sleeping peacefully after having been given his honey.

The Casino seemed as bright with lights and even more like a wedding-cake than it had the night before.

The Princess's wheel-chair was waiting for her and they passed quickly through 'The Kitchen' where the gamblers were six deep around every table.

In the *Salle Touzet* there was the same collection of magnificently be-jewelled women, and men of obvious distinction.

Almost everyone seemed to know the Princess and their progress towards the tables was considerably slowed down as people came up to speak to her.

Among them was a tall, distinguished-looking man with a small moustache, who Ancella was certain was Russian even before he spoke.

She was not mistaken.

"Good-evening, Your Imperial Highness," the Princess said. "My son greatly enjoyed his dinner with you last night."

"I am hoping that you also will honour me one evening," the Grand Duke Mikhail replied.

"You have only to ask me," the Princess answered, almost coquettishly.

The Grand Duke's eyes were on Ancella as she stood beside the Princess's chair.

After a moment he said:

"A new face in the Casino and a very lovely one! It is something of an event! Will you not introduce me?"

The Princess made a little exclamation as if she suddenly remembered Ancella's presence and said:

"May I present to Your Imperial Highness Miss Ancella Winton, my English Nurse-Companion, who has only just arrived from England?"

Ancella sank down in a deep curtsey.

"I am sure Miss Winton looks after you well," the Grand Duke said to the Princess.

"She does indeed!" the Princess replied, "and now, if Your Imperial Highness will forgive me, I must find myself a place at the Baccarat table."

The Grand Duke stood back for the wheel-chair to pass him; then, as Ancella would have followed, to her astonishment she felt his hand on her arm.

"One minute, Miss Winton," the Grand Duke said in a low voice. "I would like to talk to you. Will you join me in a glass of champagne?"

For a moment Ancella was too surprised to answer him. Then she said quickly:

"I am afraid that is impossible, Your Imperial Highness. The Princess likes me to be beside her."

"When people are gambling," the Grand Duke answered, "they are blind and deaf to everything else that goes on. Meet me later in the Bar, in about an hour's time."

"It will be impossible!" Ancella replied, but he merely smiled at her and said firmly:

"I shall be waiting!"

She turned away quickly and hurried after the Princess. The Grand Duke's invitation made her feel nervous.

Last night no-one seemed to notice her and she had somehow not expected to be anything but an anonymous figure in the glittering crowd of women that thronged the Casino.

But there had been no mistaking, even to someone as innocent as she was, the light that glittered in the Grand Duke's eyes or the manner in which he had spoken.

Ancella told herself she must be clever and on her guard, as she had no intention of involving herself with the Grand Duke.

It was not only Sir Felix and Dr. Groves who had spoken of the Russian Grand Dukes, their attractions and wild extravagances.

It was one of the many criticisms levelled against Monte Carlo that it attracted the great spenders of every country, and the Grand Dukes of Russia in particular were the most profligate and the most notorious.

As she moved towards the Baccarat table where the Princess had already been found a place, Ancella could not help looking back.

She saw the Grand Duke was standing where she had left him but he had been joined by a lady wearing a jewelled head-dress covered with pearls and bristling with ospreys.

Round her neck she wore three ropes of enormous pearls which reached almost to her knees.

Although Ancella was ignorant of the identity of the Socialites moving round the Casino, there was no mistaking, even for someone who lived in the country, the flamboyant, exotic figure of Gaby Deslys.

She was a French actress who had suddenly sprung to fame.

Even the English magazines published sketches and photographs of her, and it seemed that no-one could write about Paris without describing Gaby, her pearls and her feathered hats.

Ancella remembered what she had said to Sir Felix and could not help smiling.

"I am certainly a little English Sparrow compared with such a Bird of Paradise," she thought.

Then resolutely, as she stood behind the Princess's chair, she tried to understand the game that was being played with cards which were drawn from what was called a 'Shoe'.

The Princess had been playing for only about a quarter of an hour before the Marchioness and Prince Vladimer appeared and sat down at the other side of the table.

Ancella saw the Prince put a great deal of money down in front of the Marchioness while he contented himself with a much more modest pile.

For a moment neither of them appeared to notice the Princess. The Marchioness lifted her lovely face towards the Prince, looked at him with her blue eyes in a manner which proclaimed her intentions all too obviously.

"How can he resist anyone so beautiful?" Ancella wondered.

She thought how dull and uninteresting she must look beside the Marchioness, whose gown of silver lamé was very décolletée.

She wore a necklace of turquoises and diamonds, and long ear-rings of the same stones fell from her perfectly-shaped ears.

In her hair there was a white aigrette held with a diamond brooch and two bracelets were clasped over her long white kid-gloves which reached above her elbows.

She looked really impressive and dignified besides being so beautiful, and it struck Ancella that she was in fact exactly the right sort of wife for the Prince.

She would grace the jewels which the Princess wore and which would one day be his, and she would look her best in the huge, glittering Ball-Room of the Winter Palace, and even more lovely when, wrapped in furs, she travelled over the snow-covered land in a sleigh.

Ancella was so deep in her thoughts about the Marchioness and the Prince, even while they hurt with the unaccountable pain that she had felt at dinner, that she did not realise that the Comte André had joined the Princess until she heard her say:

"Thank Heaven you are here, André! It makes me sick to sit at the table and watch that woman opposite trying to eat up my son with her eyes."

There was a venom in the Princess's voice that was unmistakable and Comte André replied:

"Forget her. I want to talk to you."

A flunkey drew the Princess's chair from the table and as he pushed her away Ancella, who was following, saw out of the corner of her eye the Prince lift his head to watch his mother leave.

Then resolutely she looked in another direction, determined not to let him think that she was interested in what he was doing.

The Princess and the Comte went to the same Salon where they had sat the night before and almost instantly were deep in conversation.

Ancella moved towards the seat against the wall where she had sat for so many long hours the night before, and as she did so thought that in the distance she could see the Grand Duke Mikhail.

She was half-afraid that he would come to find her, thinking that she was ready to meet him as he had suggested.

Quickly, hoping she was invisible, she slipped out through the open window as she had done the previous night into the garden where she had been joined by Mr. Harnsworth.

To-night it was completely empty and there was only

the beauty of the stars and a new moon in the sky.

'Everyone will be bowing to it and turning their money,' Ancella thought with a smile, knowing that was a superstition which was certain not to be forgotten by the gamblers.

She moved slowly towards the edge of the terrace which dropped down hundreds of feet towards the sea.

There was the same sweet fragrance of lilies that she had noticed the night before and there was also music, and she recognised a slow Viennese Waltz.

She looked down at the harbour and saw not only the yachts at anchor, but also a large ship moving slowly out towards the open sea, its lights reflected in the water.

"One day you and I will be in a ship travelling towards new horizons," a deep voice said beside her.

Ancella started.

She had not heard the Prince approach, and yet now he was there it seemed to complete the perfection of the night.

"Would you come with me?" he asked.

"Where . . . to?" she enquired.

"Would it matter, if we were together?"

She could find no answer to this. She only knew her heart had started to beat violently and she felt the strange sensation he always had on her rising irresistibly until it reached her throat and it was hard to speak.

"You are even more lovely than I remember when I left you this afternoon," he said. "Did you think about me?"

"It would have been . . . impossible not to . . . do so," Ancella answered.

The words came from her lips in a whisper and she knew he was smiling as he said softly:

"That is what I hoped you would say."

"How did you . . . know I was . . . here?"

"I guessed that this is where you would come."

As if without speaking she asked the question, he went on:

"The Marchioness is winning. She will not miss me and I had to find you."

Ancella did not speak and after a moment he said:

"Do you know what an agony it is not to be beside you, not to be able to talk to you? Ever since I have known you, Ancella, you have made me suffer a thousand different emotions I have never felt before."

He paused, then he said very softly:

"I love you!"

Just for a moment it seemed to Ancella that the brilliance of the stars blinded her eyes, then she replied:

"You know . . . you should . . . not say . . . such . . . things to me . . . and you know I must not . . . listen!"

"I cannot help it!" the Prince said simply. "Look at me!"

It was a command, and obediently, without thought, Ancella turned her head.

His face was very clear in the light of the moon and when she saw the expression in his eyes it was impossible to move.

"I love you!" he said again and now the words were fierce. "I love you and I can think of nothing but you, until I wonder how long it will be before I snatch you up in my arms and carry you away where we can be alone."

"Please . . . please . . ." Ancella murmured.

She knew even as she said the words they had no meaning.

She could only stare up at him, then slowly and as smoothly as the ship which was gliding out of the harbour he drew her into his arms.

It was inevitable and she could not resist him. He held her closer and still closer against him. He looked down at her face up-turned to his, then his mouth was on hers.

For a moment Ancella was conscious only that his lips were hard, when somehow she had expected them to be

132

soft. Then like a flash of lightning the fire that she felt in him swept through her.

She felt it invade her tinglingly, thrillingly, sweeping through her relentlessly, and with it came the sudden weakness that held an emotion so exquisite and so wonderful that Ancella could no longer think, but only feel.

It was love – a love fierce, passionate, demanding, a love which belonged to eternity, and was in itself part of the divine.

It seemed that the stars, the sea, the fragrance of the flowers and the music were all part of the Prince and of her.

Everything had vanished except themselves and a beauty that made them no longer human but as gods.

The Prince's arms tightened and instinctively she drew closer to him. They were no longer two people but one, joined by a love so ecstatic that it was part of creation.

"*Douchka*, my little darling!" the Prince murmured against her lips.

Then he was kissing her again, wildly, passionately, possessively, until the very stars seemed to fall from the sky and lie at their feet.

Quite suddenly he released her.

Then without a word, as silently as he had come, he moved away and almost before Ancella realised what had happened he disappeared through a lighted window into the Casino.

She felt as if her legs would not support her and she would fall to the ground. Then she put both her hands up to her breast as if to stop the tumultuous throbbing of her heart.

She had never realised it was possible to feel as she felt at this moment, carried up into the sky, enveloped with glory, awakened to wonders which belonged to the world of the spirit.

She felt herself quiver and tremble.

Gradually she came back to reality, to the fragrance of the flowers, to the sound of the music, and the reflection of the stars on the sea.

"I must go back," she thought.

But it was impossible to move, impossible, for the moment, to return to the commonplace and the mundane when she had reached the gates of Paradise.

"I love him!" she whispered. "I love him!"

With a superhuman effort Ancella forced herself to turn round and walk towards the Casino.

She had a sudden shrinking, a physical intensity which was painful, at the idea of going back, of losing the enchantment which had swept her up to the skies.

But she thought perhaps the Princess would want her and she had no idea how long she had been in the garden.

Everything seemed to be out of focus, the only thing that was real was the throbbing of her lips on which she could still feel his.

She stepped in through the window and for a moment the lights were so bright that it was hard to see.

Then to her consternation she realised that the Princess was sitting alone in her wheel-chair, and the Comte was no longer with her.

Ancella walked quickly towards her.

"Where have you been?" the Princess asked angrily. "You are supposed to be here in attendance upon me. How dare you disappear in such a manner!"

"I am very sorry, Ma'am," Ancella replied. "I thought the Comte would be with you for a long time, and I went into the garden."

"A long time!" the Princess snorted. "What chance have I of having him for a long time with that woman giving him orders, forcing him to obey her?"

"He . . . he has left the Casino?" Ancella asked vaguely.

"He has gone back to his wife!" the Princess snapped. "He has to leave now – to-night, to reach her in Paris in the morning. She wants him. She commands him! Because he is weak, and all men are weak, he obeys!"

"I am sorry!" Ancella said.

The Princess's voice was not only angry, there was also no concealing the fact that she was suffering.

Suddenly she seemed to sink back in her wheel-chair, as if she was exhausted.

"Take me home!" she ordered. "I can stand no more!"

Ancella signalled to an attendant who hurried to the Princess's side.

"Back to the tables, Your Highness?" he asked.

"We are leaving," Ancella said before the Princess could speak. "Please take us to the door and order Her Highness's carriage."

She wondered, as they moved quickly through the *Salle Touzet* into 'The Kitchen', whether she should inform the Prince that they were leaving, but she shrank from speaking to him and she thought too that the Princess looked quite ill.

The patches of rouge on her cheeks were standing out vividly and now she appeared even older than she normally did, a shrivelled old woman with a deeply lined face which for the moment had no semblance of beauty in it.

It took only a few minutes for the carriage to be brought to the door of the Casino.

A footman and Ancella helped the Princess in. She lay back against the cushioned seat and a sable rug was put over her knees.

The horses set off, going more slowly down the hill which led to the harbour than they would do once they were on the main road.

As they journeyed the Princess began to mutter to herself:

"André, Serge, Vladimer – it is always the same! They take them from me – I cannot hold them. Whatever I say – whatever I feel – they leave me."

Ancella longed to comfort her, but she did not know what to say.

"I hate that woman – I hate her!" the Princess said suddenly with a new venom in her voice. "She has only sent for André because she knows he might be seeing me. She is jealous of me. She always has been. That *parvenue*, that American upstart who had nothing to offer a man except her dollars!"

Her head fell forward onto her chest and she muttered:

"I should have killed her long ago – then he would have been free!"

Ancella felt she could not have heard correctly!

Then, as if talking to herself, Her Highness continued:

"I was too young and too inexperienced to kill those women who tempted Serge – but I got rid of that – girl that Vladimer was to marry and that – dancer! She died!"

"What are you . . . saying?" Ancella asked, her voice smitten with a sudden horror, so that it was only a whisper.

"I killed them!" the Princess said. "Do you hear me? I saved Vladimer – as I should have saved André – long ago. That woman must – die! Boris will find a way!"

Chapter Six

When she was in bed Ancella found it impossible to sleep.

She had gone with the Princess to her bed-room where Maria was waiting, and in a low voice that could not be overheard she said to the maid:

"Her Highness is not well."

Maria glanced sharply at her employer and replied:

"I was expecting it. She always looks like this when she's been with *him*."

Ancella said good-night and, curtseying, left the Princess's bed-room; but she had an idea that it would not have mattered whether she stayed or went, for the Princess was deep in her own thoughts.

When she was in bed in the darkness Ancella found herself going over and over again what the Princess had said, feeling the shock of it, so that it was hard to think clearly.

She must have been mistaken, she told herself, she must have misunderstood what the Princess had said. It was impossible for it to be the truth.

Her Highness could not have meant that she had deliberately killed her son's fiancée or the dancer in whom he was interested.

Ancella told herself it might have been merely a figure of speech, or perhaps her mind being a trifle deranged, after they died she had imagined she had something to do with their deaths.

And yet, now Ancella thought of it, there had been – or was she imagining it? – an insinuation in Captain Sudley's voice when she had overheard him speaking of the women, when she was concealed beneath the balustrade.

"There must be a perfectly reasonable explanation for the way in which they lost their lives," she told herself.

But almost as if to refute her reasoning, she could hear again Dr. Groves telling her how fanatically possessive the Princess was and how jealous she had been, first of her husband, then of her son.

"It cannot be true . . . it cannot!" Ancella whispered in the darkness, but found herself thinking of Boris and shivering.

It was Boris who would have carried out his mistress's orders, Boris who would have been responsible for the death of the Russian girl who had died by drowning and Boris who would have pushed the ballet-dancer out of a high window.

Ancella thought of the Prince, and like the sea that becomes calm after a storm she felt the tumult within her recede and a very different emotion possess her.

Of one thing she was sure, if there had been treachery, if there had been a crime committed, the Prince would have had no part in it.

She knew that with so much certainty that, even if the Princess had told her he was a murderer, she would have proclaimed his innocence, whatever the evidence against him.

She knew irrefutably, without need of further assurance, that Prince Vladimer was himself very different from the outside world's impression of him.

To the chattering social gossips he might be a heartbreaker, a rich Russian aristocrat seeking amusement, but to her he was very different.

He was a man whom she would have trusted not only with her life, but also with her soul.

She had known when he kissed her that the fire that sprang within them both was in its very ecstasy divine.

She felt the glory of it sweep over her again, so that

she quivered, not now in fear or disgust, but with a wonder and a gratitude that came from the very depths of her heart.

"I love him!" she told herself and felt as if the words vibrated in the darkness of her small bed-room.

"I love him! I love him!"

She felt that once again they were standing beneath the stars and he was carrying her up into the sky, and that the fragrance of the flowers and the music were all a part of their love.

She had known him such a very short time, and yet she thought now he had always been there in her thoughts and was so indivisibly a part of her that they had in fact recognised each other from the moment they met.

She had been aware of it when he had spoken of love at Eza and yet she had been afraid to believe the promptings of her own heart.

She had felt then that he was sweeping her away like a flood-tide and she must struggle to retain her own identity; but now, since he had kissed her, she knew it was impossible not to accept the inevitable.

She was his, and he was hers.

She shut her eyes feeling again his mouth possessing her, and knew that nothing else was of importance save that she belonged to him and that he loved her.

It had seemed utterly unbelievable when he had told her so as they sat overlooking the sea. Until that moment they had hardly spoken more than a few sentences to each other.

But now she knew that the Prince had been right: when their eyes met in the Casino and a strange magnetism passed between them, they had found each other across eternity.

Nothing else was of any consequence and gradually the Princess's mutterings faded from Ancella's mind and she slept with a smile on her lips.

She dreamt that the Prince was holding her in his arms and her head was on his shoulder . . .

* * *

But with the morning the horror of what she had heard came back to her and as Ancella dressed she wondered whether she would be wise to send for Dr. Groves.

But even as she thought of it she shrank from relating to anyone what the Princess had said, least of all to an outsider, even if he was her Physician.

She knew she could not tell the Prince, could not bring herself to repeat what his mother had said and watch, because she would be unable to help herself, the expression in his eyes.

Had he suspected? Had he any idea what had happened to the women of whom he had been fond?

Ancella drew herself up sharply.

She was assuming that what the Princess had said was true; yet another part of her mind was convinced it was just an hallucination, and that when two accidents had happened, both of which were very welcome to Her Highness, she was prepared to believe that she herself was responsible for them.

"That is the truth!" Ancella said firmly. "If the Princess is better to-day she may not remember what she said to me and I need never think of it again."

They were brave words, but she knew it would be difficult not to remember what had been said, not to feel them haunting her, hovering at the back of her mind.

When she had dressed and had her breakfast Ancella went along to the Princess's room. Maria was in the passage outside.

"How is Her Highness this morning?"

"She had a bad night," Maria replied. "At dawn she rang for me and I gave her a sleeping draught. She is not yet awake."

"I am sorry," Ancella said. "I am afraid it upset Her

Highness when her friend the Comte had to leave."

"It always upsets her," Maria answered. "He is the only person who really remembers her as she was! So beautiful, *M'mselle*! There was not a lady in the whole Court who could hold a candle to her!"

"I can believe that," Ancella said, "and it must be hard, when you have been beautiful, to grow old."

"Beauty does not save one from suffering," Maria said sharply.

Then as if she thought she had said too much she said:

"Go for a walk in the sunshine, *M'mselle*. The Princess should be awake in half an hour or so, then she will want to see you."

Ancella was glad to escape. She was feeling nervous of seeing the Princess again in case she should remember what she had said in the carriage.

Ancella went down the long white steps into the garden.

The sunshine glittered on the fountains, and the leaves of the trees moved gently in a soft breeze from the sea.

It was very lovely and as Ancella walked towards the balustrade at the end of the promontory, she saw there was someone already there.

For a moment she hesitated, then her heart seemed to turn over in her breast and she went forward eagerly.

Only as she reached him did the Prince turn from his contemplation of the sea.

"Ancella!"

The way he spoke her name was an embrace in itself.

She looked up at him, her eyes shining, her lips parted a little at the excitement of seeing him.

"I was thinking of you," he said. "I keep wondering, my darling, what you have done to me."

It was difficult to speak but somehow Ancella found her voice.

"I was . . . thinking about you . . . last night."

"I thought you must be," the Prince said. "Oh, my

sweet, I did not know anything could be so wonderful or so magical as that moment when I touched your lips."

His eyes met Ancella's and she felt, although he did not move, as if he kissed her again.

He looked at her for a long moment before he said:

"I must not stay here talking to you, as I am sure you understand. I will find out what everyone is doing, and perhaps we can meet this afternoon."

He saw her eyes light up and there was no need for words. She knew by the expression in his face what he was feeling.

He turned with what was an obvious effort and walked back towards the Villa.

Ancella held on to the grey stone of the balustrade.

She was trembling with an ecstasy which made her body feel as weak as when he had held her close to him and she felt as if she melted not only into his arms but also into his body, mind and soul.

"I love him!" she whispered beneath her breath.

The waves lapping gently beneath her seemed to repeat the words over and over again.

"I love him! I love him!"

When Ancella went back to the Villa and up to the Princess's room she saw Boris coming through the door and felt, as she always did, a revulsion at the sight of him.

This morning there was a faint smile on his thick lips and his hooded eyes seemed more sinister than ever. She thought that he was pleased about something, and felt instinctively that he was the purveyor of bad news.

As he passed her he seemed to exude evil and she felt herself shrink away from him as if he might contaminate her.

There was no sign of Maria, and Ancella knocked at the Princess's door.

As she entered it was to find the Princess sitting up in bed. The moment she looked at her Ancella knew that

142

she was in the same agitated state that she had been in the night before.

"Oh, it is you, is it?" she said almost rudely. "Well, perhaps you can confirm what Boris has just told me."

"Confirm what, Ma'am?" Ancella asked, moving towards the bed.

"That the Marchioness has snared my son, as she always intended to do."

"What do you . . . mean?" Ancella asked.

She felt as she spoke as if a cold hand clutched at her heart.

"Boris tells me," the Princess said, "that after everyone had returned from the Casino last night, she went to his bed-room."

"I do not . . . believe it!"

Before she could prevent herself Ancella heard her voice ring out.

"It is true!" the Princess answered. "Boris is never mistaken. She has been stalking him – that blue-eyed English harlot! I have watched her doing it. Smarming over him, touching him with her hands, looking into his eyes, inviting him to possess her, and now she has succeeded!"

Ancella stood as if she was turned to stone, the blood drained away from her face and she was very pale.

The Princess was not looking at her and after a moment in a voice that she hardly recognised as her own Ancella managed to say:

"There must be some . . . mistake! I am absolutely . . . convinced that His Highness is not . . . interested in the Marchioness in that . . . way."

"But she is interested in him!" the Princess snarled. "And what man ever resists temptation?"

She paused for a moment, then went on:

"They are all the same! Serge, André, Vladimer. When a pretty woman beckons they follow. Not that Vladimer had to go anywhere – she went to him!"

Ancella thought she was going to faint.

With an effort she forced herself to walk to the window, trying to breathe deeply and fighting the darkness that seemed to be creeping into her mind so that it was hard to think.

"I will get rid of her!" the Princess said from behind her. "She shall not stay in this Villa – I will not have it! As I have told Vladimer before, I will not play hostess to his lights of love!"

Ancella held onto the lintel of the window.

'I must not . . . faint . . . I must not let the . . . Princess know,' she thought frantically.

"Shall I order Your Highness's luncheon in bed?" Maria's voice asked from the door.

"In bed? I am not staying in bed!" the Princess retorted. "I am going downstairs. I want to see what is happening!"

"You'd do much better taking a rest," Maria said. "You're tired out, Your Highness. Stay here."

"I will do nothing of the sort!" the Princess replied. "Besides, His Imperial Highness is coming to luncheon. He has asked himself and I must be downstairs to receive him."

"The Grand Duke would understand if he knew Your Highness was ill," Maria expostulated.

"I am not ill!" the Princess insisted. "Besides, Royalty is Royalty, as you well know, Maria, although why the Grand Duke wishes to have luncheon with us I cannot imagine!"

Ancella heard the Princess talking as if she was very far away, but her faintness was passing and after a few moments she was able to turn round.

"Is there . . . anything I can do for . . . Your Highness?" she asked.

"Nothing!" the Princess replied, then changed her mind. "You can read to me while I am getting dressed. I had better keep up with world affairs and you will find in the local paper a list of the latest arrivals in Monte Carlo. We do not want to miss anybody of interest!"

The Princess was speaking now in quite a normal voice but there was a strange look in her eyes which was one almost of excitement.

Ancella had the uneasy feeling that she was plotting something, and yet, she asked herself, why should she care?

After all the Prince had said, after all she had thought that kiss had meant, the Marchioness had gone to his room and he must have allowed her to stay there.

Had he compelled her to leave immediately, Ancella was sure Boris would have reported it, and she wondered with a feeling that was one of despair how long they had been together.

Had he kissed those beautiful wild-rose lips? Had he said to the Marchioness the same things he had said to her?

Everything in her body cried out at the thought of it. Her whole being seemed to revolt at his duplicity.

And yet, she told herself, she must face facts. The Marchioness had been determined to become his mistress. She had heard her say so the first day she had arrived, and now apparently without much difficulty she had succeeded.

To Ancella the Princess's revelations had been like a dagger which was plunged into her heart. For the moment she was numb with the shock of it. She could not even feel the pain that she expected.

She only felt as if she was moving in a dark fog and she was no longer herself, no more than a puppet who walked and talked but had become completely unhuman.

She picked up the newspaper and read it to the Princess, but she had not the slightest idea what she read.

Her lips said one thing but her mind was far away, desolate and alone in a barren wilderness, crying for a lost ideal.

When the Princess was dressed it was time to go downstairs for luncheon, and Ancella wondered if she should say that she had a headache and ask if she could go to her bed-room.

Then she thought that might draw attention to herself, which was the last thing she wanted.

She wished only to be anonymous, to hide if it were possible under a stone or in the darkest cave and know that no-one would seek for her or be aware of her very existence.

As she dressed, the Princess's mood had changed.

Now she was like a soldier, Ancella thought, going into battle and the glitter of excitement she had seen in her eyes was a hard, almost brutal determination to destroy what had offended her.

She noticed that Maria looked at her employer as if in perplexity.

And Ancella thought too, as the Princess put on her usual fantastic amount of jewellery, that she did it as if her gems were an armour with which she protected herself against a dangerous foe.

Finally, with two long ropes of pearls around her neck and diamonds glittering in her ears and on her fingers, the Princess was ready.

"Come, Miss Winton," she said.

It was somehow a battle call.

"I don't know what Your Highness is up to," Maria muttered, "but don't you go upsetting yourself. Boris has no right to come here disturbing you with his tales and his sneaky goings-on, as I've told him often enough."

"Boris does what he is told to do," the Princess replied.

There was something in the way she spoke which made Ancella shudder.

Could the Princess have really told Boris to drown one woman and throw another from a high window?

All the shock of what she felt while they drove back from the Casino swept over Ancella again.

Then because she felt too weak to protest or do anything

other than was expected she followed the Princess down to the Salon.

It was not as large a party as there had been last night, but already the guests staying in the house were assembled and Ancella saw the Prince standing in the window talking to a very tall, beautiful woman.

As soon as the Princess appeared he brought her across and said:

"Mama, I am sure you remember the Duchess of Marlborough?"

"Of course," the Princess said holding out her hand. "How delightful to see you again."

"It is a great pleasure to be here," the Duchess answered in French but with the suspicion of an American accent.

Ancella remembered that she had once been one of the rich Vanderbilts and her marriage to the Duke had been reported in every newspaper.

"May I introduce Miss Ancella Winton?" the Prince asked the Duchess.

As he spoke Ancella thought his voice softened but as she dropped a curtsey she told herself she hated him.

How could he speak like that when he had betrayed everything she believed in, everything which in her stupidity and ignorance she had thought was from God and a part of Heaven itself?

Two more people were announced and the Prince was obliged to turn away. Then Ancella heard the Butler say to him:

'The carriage of His Imperial Highness is coming down the drive, Your Highness!"

The Prince hurried to the front door to receive the Grand Duke. When he entered the Salon the ladies all sank down in a deep curtsey.

He kissed the Princess's hand, then his eyes sought Ancella and she knew the reason he had invited himself for luncheon.

She was well aware that he had a wife and a family living in Russia, and that the actress who had been with him at the Casino was only one of the many notorious women with whom his name had been associated.

"Russians are all the same!" she told herself bitterly. "Prince Vladimer is no different from the rest."

She had the feeling that the Grand Duke was manoeuvring so that he could speak to her and deliberately she moved closer to the Princess, as if ready to help her to her feet when luncheon was announced.

Ancella was naturally some way down the table from the Grand Duke and from Prince Vladimer and she hoped that she could sit in silence and no-one would notice her.

It was impossible for her to eat anything and she sipped only a little of the white wine that was poured into her glass because she was afraid that once again she might feel faint.

It was difficult to concentrate, hard to understand the conversation that was going on all around her. The guests might have been talking Hindustani.

And she knew that it was impossible for her to look at the Marchioness.

But even so she was aware that her voice seemed gayer than anyone else's, her tinkling laughter ringing out continually.

"She is happy!" Ancella told herself and felt again she was in a wilderness and utterly alone.

The meal seemed to drag on, course succeeding course. The Grand Duke was telling anecdotes which made everyone laugh.

Suddenly Ancella heard him say:

"There is a new system this year which I had not heard of previously."

"What is that?" the Princess asked.

"I thought you were sure to have heard of it," the Grand

Duke replied. "Perhaps you have. It is a system of staking on the meaning of one's name rather than the name itself."

"Do you mean adding up the number of letters in our names?" the Marchioness asked. "We have all tried that. I believe it only works the first time you play."

"What a mantologist was explaining to me last night," the Grand Duke replied, "is that the subtlety lies in knowing the meaning of the name. It is affiliated with the Zodiac and hyperphysics. Anyway, Mikhail is seven. I backed it on her insistence and I must admit it turned up an amazing number of times."

"But how do we know what our names mean?" the Duchess of Marlborough enquired.

"Apparently all names have a meaning," the Grand Duke replied. "Prince Frederich was with me. His name in old German means 'peaceful Chieftain'. That adds up to seventeen, and sure enough that number came up four times at one table."

"How exciting!" the Duchess exclaimed. "But I have no idea what my name, Consuelo, means."

"There must be a book of names somewhere in Monte Carlo," the Grand Duke said with a smile.

"I am quite sure it will not include Feodogrova!" the Princess exclaimed irritably.

"I should think it unlikely," the Grand Duke answered, "but Alexandra, which I believe is Your Highness's second name, in the Greek means 'defender'."

"Eight!" the Princess said excitedly. "I shall back it the entire evening!"

"My name is Helen," one of the guests said. "What does that mean?"

"Helen is Greek and means 'bright'," the Grand Duke replied, "and Ancella, also Greek, means 'angel'."

It seemed to Ancella that everyone turned to look at her and she felt the blood rising in her cheeks.

Even as she did so she saw Captain Sudley stare at her from the other side of the table with an almost incredulous expression on his face.

Then his eyes narrowed!

Still talking excitedly about numbers, the ladies left the Dining-Room, and as if she had no longer any interest in her guests the Princess excused herself, saying she must rest.

Grateful not to have encountered the Grand Duke again, Ancella followed her employer upstairs.

She told herself there was no reason why anyone should connect her with the story Captain Sudley had told about his friend, Mr. Harnsworth.

At the same time she was frightened.

Then with a sudden determination she told herself it was of no consequence. She would go home to England and the sooner she left the better.

It would be impossible to stay on, loving the Prince and knowing he had betrayed her.

"I must get hold of a book of names," the Princess was saying. "A groom can ride into Monte Carlo."

She paused for a moment then she said:

"It is a good thing the Marchioness did not ask what her name means! I assure you I should have thought of something very appropriate!"

The venom was back in her voice.

"Come and have your rest," Maria suggested. "If you're gambling again to-night Your Highness'll be exhausted if you don't have your proper sleep."

"I have things to think about," the Princess said evasively.

"There's no point in worrying your head about His Highness," Maria admonished. "He's grown up. He can do what he wants. All mothers, and Your Highness is no exception, have to realise that sooner or later!"

"I will not have it!" the Princess said angrily. "I will

not have it, Maria! I do not like her. I never have liked her! She has been trying to get him ever since she came here."

"It's nothing serious – you can be sure of that!" Maria said soothingly. "Men will be men, as women have found since the beginning of time."

Ancella felt she could bear no more.

"Men will be men!"

And the Prince, who she had thought was different, was no better than any other man.

Like Captain Sudley, who would accept money from the woman he loved. Like the Grand Duke, whose wife was left behind in Russia while he enjoyed himself in Monte Carlo. Like the Prince of Wales, with his constant unfaithfulness to his lovely Danish wife.

They were all the same.

"Men were men!"

She had been a fool to expect anything different!

And yet she felt as if her whole body was weeping bitter tears at the discovery.

When she went to her room she sat in a chair, put her face in her hands and wondered if it was possible to suffer such agony without dying from it.

How long she sat there she had no idea, but she was startled by a knock on the door.

"What is it?" she asked.

"Will you go down to the Salon, *M'mselle*?" a servant asked in French.

Ancella wanted to refuse. If it was the Prince who wanted to see her, she could not bear to speak to him; and if it was anyone else, she had nothing to say.

Then she told herself she was employed to obey orders. If she was sent for, it was a command, not a request.

"In two minutes," she replied.

"Merci, M'mselle."

She rose to her feet and walked to the mirror.

She looked at her reflection. She half expected to look old and wrinkled and that her hair would have turned white.

Instead she saw a pale face looking out at her with eyes dark with suffering, but otherwise it was very young and very vulnerable.

Automatically Ancella tidied her hair, shook the full skirts of her lilac cotton gown and turned to leave the room.

As she did so she told herself that, if indeed it was the Prince who wished to talk to her, she would inform him that she had received bad news from England and must return there immediately.

There was a post that arrived at the Villa at about two o'clock.

She could say there had been a letter which made it imperative for her to go home.

He might argue, he might try to persuade her to stay, but Ancella knew she would be strong enough not to listen to him and that no arguments, no pleadings would make her change her mind.

She drew a deep breath, then holding her head high and walking deliberately slowly she went along the corridor and down the staircase into the Hall.

The footman opened the door into the Salon, and as it closed behind her Ancella saw it was not the Prince, as she had expected, but the Marchioness who was waiting for her.

For a moment Ancella felt she could not speak with the woman who had, although she was not aware of it, been instrumental in destroying her happiness – the 'Fool's Paradise' in which she had dwelt for a short while.

Then she told herself that, whatever the Marchioness might do, she must behave like a lady.

Ancella walked towards the older woman and when she

152

reached her she dropped, as would be expected, a small respectful curtsey.

"I wanted to speak to you, Miss Winton," the Marchioness said in a low voice, "but not here because, as I am sure you know, our conversation might be overheard."

Ancella did not reply and the Marchioness continued:

"We will go into the garden. All the guests have gone and we shall be alone."

Ancella wanted to refuse, but it was impossible to do anything except follow in the wake of the Marchioness as she walked through the open French window onto the terrace and started to descend the marble steps.

She was wearing one of her favourite blue gowns and as she stepped out into the sunshine she opened her sun-shade which matched her dress and was embellished with bunches of pink rose-buds.

She appeared lovely and very Junoesque.

On reaching the garden she paused in the shade of the nearest tree to turn towards Ancella.

There was something autocratic and at the same time very elegant about her. And because she was so beautiful Ancella could not prevent the thought that she was eminently suitable to grace any position the Prince might offer her.

"I wanted to speak to you, Miss Winton," the Marchioness said in a hard voice, "because Captain Sudley has remembered that he saw you the night before last with his friend, Mr. Harnsworth."

Ancella was still. She did not answer. She only thought unhappily that this was what she might have expected.

"Mr. Harnsworth said it was an angel that helped him," the Marchioness continued. "I feel there can be no point in your denying that you were the 'angel' in question."

"I was able to . . . help Mr. Harnsworth," Ancella said after a moment, "because he was in a desperate situation

. . . and without money both he and his wife would have
. . . died. It was something which might never happen
again."

"Nevertheless, we will certainly try to see if it does," the
Marchioness said.

"I am afraid that is impossible," Ancella replied. "I
cannot help you. In fact I can help no-one else."

"How can you be sure?" the Marchioness asked. "I
understand you had never been in Monte Carlo until the
other evening. It must have been the first time you had
gambled."

"Which is I imagine, the reason I won!" Ancella said
quickly. "It is an old superstition, as His Imperial Highness said at luncheon."

"I think personally it was something more than that,"
the Marchioness said. "Perhaps you are clairvoyant, but
anyway, I wish you to play for me and try to anticipate the
numbers as you did the other evening."

"I am sorry," Ancella said, "but I cannot do that."

"You will do it!" the Marchioness replied fiercely, "and
you will do it now! This is your time off, Miss Winton, as I
have already ascertained. We will drive to Monte Carlo
and we will play Roulette until you have to return."

Ancella did not answer and she went on:

"There will be no reason for anyone else to know what
we are doing, except of course Captain Sudley who will
come with us. You will find that if you are fey, or clairvoyant, or whatever it is, it will work as well for me as for
anyone else."

"I am sorry," Ancella said again, "but I am not going
to the Casino with you, nor do I intend to play Roulette
ever again!"

"If that is your attitude," the Marchioness said slowly,
"then I shall go upstairs at once and tell the Princess what
we know. You are well aware what Her Highness is like
when it comes to gambling. She would make your life a

misery! She would tear you in pieces rather than think you were holding out on her with a system by which she could be a winner."

There was something very unpleasant in the Marchioness's voice and Ancella stiffened. At the same time she knew the Marchioness was speaking the truth.

The Princess's obsession with gambling was indisputable.

It was a good thing, Ancella thought to herself, that she was leaving.

It would be better for her to be in England with her aunts than to suffer as she was suffering here, first from the Prince and now from being blackmailed by this woman whom she disliked and despised.

She looked at the Marchioness defiantly and said quietly:

"You must do as you think right. All I can promise you is that I have no intention of visiting the Casino this afternoon with Your Ladyship or at any other time!"

As she spoke she turned to walk towards the steps.

"Now listen to me, Miss Winton . . ." the Marchioness said furiously.

Then with an effort she changed the tone of her voice and added:

"This could be to the advantage of both of us – to you as well as to me. I will provide the capital with which we will gamble and you can keep a quarter of the winnings."

"I am not interested," Ancella replied.

"Then what can I offer you?" the Marchioness enquired.

"Nothing!"

Ancella spoke a little louder than she intended. Now she had reached the steps but as she was about to climb them the Marchioness caught hold of her wrist.

"Listen to me, you little fool!" she said angrily. "I want your help and I can not believe that you do not require money. We will go to the Casino and we will try to see if the luck which was yours the other night will work again. I believe it will!"

"I have already given you my answer," Ancella replied.

She tried to move forward but the Marchioness held on to her so that she was prevented from doing so.

"Please let me go!" Ancella said coldly. "Nothing you can say or do . . . nothing . . . will make me alter my mind!"

She saw an expression of anger in the Marchioness's blue eyes which seemed to contort her face.

As if she could bear no more, Ancella struggled to release her wrist, but the Marchioness's fingers tightened.

For a moment they defied each other, then suddenly there was a scream from the terrace.

They both looked up and there, to Ancella's astonishment, at the top of the steps stood the Princess!

She was wearing the elaborate négligée of satin and lace that she wore in her bed-room, and Ancella thought that she must have walked down the stairs, for there was no sign of her wheel-chair or of a footman in attendance.

She was holding a letter in her hand. She held it up and, looking at the Marchioness, she screamed:

"How dare you say you are going to marry my son! It is not true, I tell you. He would never marry you – never! You are nothing but a strumpet, a woman without morals and I will kill you rather than allow you to possess him!"

The Princess's voice, frantic, high and hysterical, rang out, and now the Marchioness released her hold of Ancella's wrist to retort:

"What are you doing with my letter? How dare you read it. You have no right . . ."

"I have every right!" the Princess stormed. "What you have written is lies – lies, do you hear? You are a harlot and a liar and you will leave here at once!"

As she spoke she stepped forward as if to descend the steps and confront the Marchioness with what she held in her hand, then as she did so she swayed.

Just for a moment she seemed to struggle against falling, before she lost her balance and crashed down on the marble steps.

She rolled forward, her body gathering impetus until as she screamed and screamed again the Princess rolled from the bottom step to lie at the Marchioness's feet!

Chapter Seven

Ancella was awoken by Maria coming into her bed-room.

She sat up with a start.

"The Princess . . . ?" she began.

"Her Highness died two hours ago," Maria answered and crossing the room pulled back the curtains.

"I should have been . . . there," Ancella said.

"His Highness did not wish it, *M'mselle,*" Maria answered. "The Doctor was with her, but there was nothing we could do. She never regained consciousness."

Maria's voice broke and she wiped her eyes.

In the morning light Ancella could see that she had been crying desperately and her eyes were swollen.

"I am so sorry," she said rather helplessly.

There was indeed nothing she could say. The Princess had seemed dead when they picked her up from the foot of the marble steps and carried her up to her bed-room.

Then Ancella had found herself involved in a nightmare of activity.

A groom had been sent to find the Prince, who had left the Villa with the Grand Duke. Another called the Doctor and there seemed to be servants, guests and people asking innumerable questions for which Ancella had no answers.

Only the Marchioness disappeared and Ancella had not seen her again. Maria had taken charge of the letter which the Princess was holding in her hand when she fell down the steps.

Ancella had not been able to read the contents of the letter but she had noticed with it another slip of paper and saw that it was a cheque.

Almost without conscious thought she read the cheque with her eyes while her mind was still occupied over the limp body of the Princess.

Only when she was alone, after Dr. Groves had sent her to bed saying there was nothing more she could do, did she remember that the cheque had been signed by the Prince and was for £1,000.

She had been too distressed and exhausted last night to find an explanation for his giving the Marchioness such a large sum.

All she knew, all she could think of, was the Princess's voice crying out that he and the Marchioness were to be married, and each word had been like a dagger in her heart.

"So this is what the Prince had intended all the time," Ancella told herself, "and the secrecy as regards his love for me was only because he wished to conceal it from the Marchioness – not from his mother!"

The idea seemed to strip her of her pride as well as of her happiness.

How could she have been so foolish, so naive, as to think that the Prince meant anything else but to make her his mistress? The rapture she had felt and which she had believed he too experienced had only been an illusion.

She had been warned. Dr. Groves had warned her very clearly, but she had not listened.

It seemed to Ancella at that moment that she went down into a very dark hell of her own where her ideals lay smashed around her and she was humiliated to the point when everything she had believed in, everything she had ever loved, seemed worthless and tawdry.

"How could I have been so foolish?" she asked herself over and over again, knowing there was no answer except a despair that was past tears.

She must have lain for hours suffering to the point when her whole body and mind seemed wracked with pain. Then because she was exhausted she had fallen asleep.

Now sitting up in bed the events of yesterday came rushing back to her, and yet for the moment she tried not to think of herself but of Maria. The old maid, she knew, would miss the Princess with an intensity that would not be experienced by anyone else.

"I am so sorry, Maria," she said again.

"It was that wicked Boris," Maria replied furiously. "Always making trouble, always upsetting Her Highness with the things he told her."

"It was . . . he who took her the . . . letter?" Ancella asked.

"It was a letter written by Her Ladyship which she had left on the hall-table to be posted. He steamed it open as he has done so often before, and when he saw what it contained, he hurried upstairs to show it to Her Highness."

Even, for Ancella, to think of the letter and what it had revealed to the Princess was to feel again that stabbing pain.

"He is wicked – evil!" Maria was saying. "I've always hated him, *M'mselle*. And he hates me!"

Because she could not help it, Ancella found herself whispering the question that was uppermost in her mind.

"Her Highness . . . told me," she faltered, "that Boris . . . drowned the girl who was engaged to Prince . . . Vladimer. Is . . . that true?"

Maria shook her head.

"He caused the Princess to think so because he wished to please her; just as he told her – the liar – that he pushed the ballet-dancer in whom His Highness was interested out of the window."

"It was not . . . true?" Ancella asked.

"Indeed it was not!" Maria answered. "The Princess Natasha was swimming with friends in the sea. They were making a great deal of noise and did not realise she had

160

cramp. When they tried to rescue her it was too late – she had drowned!"

"A . . . and the dancer?"

It was wrong, Ancella knew, to be so inquisitive, and yet she had to know.

"It was an accident! The other actors told the Prince what had really happened and Boris was nowhere near the theatre at the time!"

Ancella drew in a deep breath.

"But because he must always boast and try to gain the Princess's favour, he told her a lot of lies about what he had done."

Maria's voice was contemptuous.

"Sometimes she would not believe him and laughed at him behind his back," she went on. " 'He talks big and does little, Maria,' she would say. But when she was upset and distressed she would want to believe him and then she would talk wildly, saying that she had ordered Boris to do such things and he had obeyed her."

"I understand what you are telling me, Maria," Ancella said gently.

"If I'd known what you heard Her Highness say, I'd have told you sooner. I've listened often enough."

Maria's voice broke again and it seemed as if she would burst into tears. But with an effort she said:

"I came to tell you, *M'mselle*, that Dr. Groves has learnt that your friend, Sir Felix Johnson, arrived in Cannes last night to be in attendance on His Royal Highness the Prince of Wales."

"Sir Felix!" Ancella exclaimed.

"Before Her Highness died Dr. Groves sent a groom to ask Sir Felix to attend her. He should be arriving soon, but it's too late!"

"I must get up," Ancella said. "Thank you for telling me. Has everyone else left?"

161

She rose as she spoke, remembering that yesterday, after the Princess's fall, the guests in the Villa had begun to leave.

"They've all gone!" Maria answered. "Her Ladyship and Captain Sudley left last. They went to stay with His Imperial Highness the Grand Duke Mikhail."

"That is where I thought they would go," Ancella answered.

Late last night the Major Domo had brought her a note.

"What is it?" she asked.

She had only left the Princess's room for a few minutes and he had been waiting for her on the landing outside.

"It is from His Imperial Highness, *M'mselle*," the Major Domo replied. "It came at the same time as one addressed to His Highness. A groom is waiting for an answer."

Ancella opened the envelope. Inside was a note written in a bold, strong hand. She read:

"Because of the tragic accident to the Princess I have invited all the guests from the Villa d'Azar to stay with me. This of course includes a certain lovely lady whose name means 'angel'. I am hoping – most fervently – she will accept my invitation. Mikhail of Russia."

Ancella read with some surprise what was written. Then, realising the Major Domo was waiting, she said:

"Will you ask the groom to inform His Imperial Highness that Miss Winton thanks him for his invitation, but is returning to England immediately?"

And that, Ancella told herself now, was what she must do.

"Will you tell the footman to bring me my trunks?" she said to Maria. "If the maids are busy, I will pack them myself."

"You are going home, *M'mselle*?"

"Yes, Maria."

"And I shall be going home with Her Highness," Maria

said with a sob. "She will be buried in St. Petersburg beside Prince Serge. Then I shall have to look for somewhere to live."

As if the idea was too much for her, Maria, with the tears running down her cheeks, went from Ancella's room, closing the door behind her.

Ancella made a movement as if she would go after the old maid and try to comfort her, but knew there was nothing she could do.

Maria had been so long with the Princess. They had been very close to each other, the two old women, enjoying their bickering and arguing, and yet, Ancella knew, having a deep affection for each other.

Now for Maria there was only the emptiness of old age without a companion. Perhaps loneliness was harder to endure than bereavement.

"Just as . . . I shall be . . . alone," Ancella said to herself.

She dressed, and having nothing black to wear put on the plainest of her white muslin gowns.

She felt, however, as she went downstairs that she should be more sombre.

Then just as she reached the Hall a carriage drew up outside. She saw Sir Felix step out and ran eagerly towards him.

"Oh, Sir Felix, I am so glad you have come!"

"I came as soon as I could," he answered. "Is the Princess still alive?"

Ancella shook her head.

"She died several hours ago."

"Then I am too late," Sir Felix said simply.

Ancella turned to the Major Domo.

"Will you inform Dr. Groves that Sir Felix Johnson has arrived?"

She drew Sir Felix into the Salon.

"Dr. Groves explained to me in his letter there had been a tragic accident," Sir Felix said. "I am sorry, my dear. I certainly did not wish to involve you in anything so unpleasant."

"It could not be helped," Ancella replied.

She was determined not to tell Sir Felix what had actually occurred.

There was no point, she thought, now that the Princess was dead, in burdening anyone with the unsavoury details.

Sir Felix walked to the open window and looked out over the terrace.

"It is very beautiful here."

"It is lovely!" Ancella agreed.

"I thought of you resting in the sun and I hoped it was doing you good," Sir Felix said. "Perhaps I can find you another post. If not, I will take you back with me when I return to England."

"I would like to do that," Ancella replied.

As she spoke the door opened and the Prince came in.

Although Ancella told herself in the night that they could never mean anything to each other again, she could not help her heart giving a sudden leap as if it turned a somersault in her breast.

He was looking a little strained, but otherwise so amazingly attractive that it was difficult to believe that wittingly or unwittingly such a terrible tragedy had revolved around him.

"It was extremely kind of you to come, Sir Felix," the Prince said holding out his hand.

"I am only sorry to learn that I am too late to be of any use, Your Highness," Sir Felix replied.

"My mother died peacefully and without being conscious of what had occurred," the Prince said.

"I can only offer my deepest sympathy," Sir Felix answered.

"Thank you."

The Prince looked at Ancella but she would not meet his eyes.

"I was just saying to Lady Ancella," Sir Felix said, "that I can take her back to England with me as soon as His Royal Highness can dispense with my services!"

He saw the surprise in the Prince's face and said hastily:

"I forgot! I sent Lady Ancella here because she was in need of rest and sun, and we thought it wisest for her to be employed under another name. She is in fact the daughter of the late Earl of Medwin."

"What I was going to suggest was something rather different," the Prince said. "I have already been in touch with a cousin of my father's, who lives at Grasse. I have asked her to come here and stay with Miss Winton – or, as you now tell me, Lady Ancella – while I convey my mother's coffin to Russia."

Ancella was very still. She could not look at the Prince as he went on:

"Immediately on my return we will be married quietly. I feel it would be a comfort for my future wife if you also could see your way, Sir Felix, to keep her company while she is waiting for me and, as an old friend, to be present at the wedding ceremony."

As the Prince finished speaking Ancella made a little sound that was actually a repressed cry. Then she walked to the window to stand with her back to the room.

As if he sensed the tension that suddenly existed between them, Sir Felix said tactfully:

"I thank Your Highness for the invitation and I think that if I play truant towards my London patients by making His Royal Highness the excuse, it might be possible for me to accept it. Now I think I should see Dr. Groves who, I understand, is upstairs."

"He is waiting for you," the Prince answered, opening the door for Sir Felix to pass into the Hall.

He shut the door and came back into the room.

He moved into the centre of it and said quietly:

"Ancella, my precious, come here!"

She did not move and after a moment he walked a little nearer to her.

"I want to talk to you."

With an effort Ancella found her voice.

"Why did you . . . tell Sir Felix we are to be . . . married?"

"Because we are," the Prince answered simply.

She did not answer and after a moment he said:

"Can it be possible that you have really been upset by what you thought was meant in the letter which was instrumental in killing my mother? Surely you did not believe such a lie?"

"Was . . . it a . . . lie?" Ancella asked almost beneath her breath.

"I thought that you trusted me," the Prince said.

"I . . . did!" Ancella replied. "But . . ."

She turned as she spoke and the expression on the Prince's face made her heart start beating wildly.

"I told you before, my darling," he said. "There are no 'buts' between us."

There was a silence.

Ancella knew the Prince was waiting for her to speak, yet for a moment she could not find words to express the misery and bewilderment she felt.

Then the words seemed to burst from her lips.

"But . . . she . . . she went to your . . . room? You . . . gave her that . . . huge cheque?"

Ancella held her breath. She felt as if the whole world was still waiting for the Prince's answer before he said:

"When we first met, you told me that when you helped the man who was in deep distress in the Casino you had a conviction as to what number would turn up. Was that not true?"

"Y . . yes," Ancella murmured, wondering where the conversation was leading.

"I want you to use that sixth sense now," the Prince

166

said, "the clairvoyance that will give you a 'conviction' where I am concerned."

He paused, then he said:

"Look at me, Ancella!"

She knew he was waiting with his eyes on hers, and yet somehow she could not look into his face.

"Look at me!" he repeated masterfully.

Almost reluctantly she raised her worried grey eyes to his.

"Now answer me truthfully and from the very depths of your heart," the Prince said softly. "Do you trust me?"

His eyes held hers like a magnet.

She could feel the strange spell that she had experienced when they first met creep over her, so that it was impossible to move, almost impossible to breathe.

She knew he was waiting and after a moment she whispered:

"Yes . . yes!"

"And you love me?"

"Yes."

"You are sure about that? You are utterly and completely convinced in your heart and in your soul that you belong to me and I belong to you?"

There was a light in Ancella's eyes that had not been there before.

Now she understood what he was saying!

She did love him! She did trust him and she knew irrefutably that they belonged to each other.

All the misery, all the doubt that had been hers during the night, had gone. And just as she had done in the garden of the Casino she moved towards him seeking the comfort, the protection and the safety of his arms.

He held her very close and while she waited and longed for him to kiss her, he said:

"You are quite sure, my beautiful darling? The conviction is really there?"

167

"I am sure . . . absolutely . . . sure!" Ancella said. "How could I have thought anything else . . . and yet I was . . . afraid I had . . . lost you."

"You could never lose me!" the Prince said. "As I told you when we were at Eza, we have been together since the beginning of time and we will be together through eternity."

She felt herself quiver because of the depth and sincerity in his voice. Then he said:

"I want you to forget what happened yesterday. It was something you should never have experienced. I deeply regret that you have been hurt and distressed as I know you have. Will you forgive me for any part I may have had in it?"

"There is . . . nothing to . . . forgive!" Ancella murmured and meant it.

"The Marchioness was in debt," the Prince said. "She came to my room to ask for my help and, because I had found her attractive until I saw you, I gave her a thousand pounds."

He paused before he continued:

"I have seen the very stupid letter she wrote to the firm which was about to sue her, telling them that the rest of the money she owed would be sent to them when she married, which she intended to do very shortly."

His voice had a note of anger in it as he went on:

"As she enclosed the cheque I had signed, it was obvious they would draw the conclusion from her letter that I was the man she was to marry – as my mother did."

Ancella hid her face against his shoulder.

"I am . . . ashamed! But I . . . did not . . . understand."

"How could you be expected to, my innocent darling?" he asked. "You are so young, so unversed in the intrigues, subterfuge and falsehoods of the Social world. That is why I have a plan to suggest to you."

There was something in his tone that made Ancella

raise her head to look up at him wide-eyed.

"What is . . . it? " she asked.

"Nothing frightening," he said reassuringly. "It is just that, because I feel that angels are out of place, not only in Monte Carlo but also in St. Petersburg, Paris and London, I want to take you away."

He felt Ancella draw in a quick breath of excitement.

"Not just for a short while, my precious love," he said, "but for years, perhaps for the rest of our lives."

Ancella did not speak and he went on:

"I own a considerable amount of land in America – in Florida, as it happens – and because I want to do something worthwhile in my life and not just waste time in the pleasure-spots of Europe, I want to develop that land and build a house there for myself and for my wife."

His arms tightened as he went on:

"When I saw you in the Tavern holding that baby in your arms I thought Florida would be a fine place to bring up our children. There are new ideas, new inventions, a new way of life to be found across the Atlantic. Shall we leave the old world behind, my lovely *douchka* and seek new horizons together? "

There was a radiance in Ancella's face that he had never seen before and it made her even more beautiful.

"You know it would be like . . . Heaven to be . . . anywhere with you!" she said. "Here I am . . . frightened . . . because you are so . . . important and I am so ignorant of your sort of life. I might fail you."

"You would never do that," the Prince said.

"But in America I could work with you . . . look after you . . . help you . . . and love you," Ancella whispered.

"That is what I want," he replied. "That is what I have longed for all the years when I have been trying to find you."

He looked down into her eyes.

"My convictions told me that somewhere in the world

there was the woman who was the other part of me. How could I have known, how could I have guessed, she was – an angel?"

Ancella gave a little laugh, then the Prince's lips were on hers and she felt, as she had the night before, that he was sweeping her up into the sky.

Once again the sunshine, the sky, the flowers, the sea, everything which was beautiful and wonderful was a part of them.

Ancella felt the Prince's kiss grow more demanding, more passionate and she felt as if he awoke a flame within her which seeped its way through her so that not only her love was his but her body, her heart and her soul.

As he held her closer she knew that love was not only gentleness and beauty; it was also a tempest, a fire, a whirlwind, so majestic, so overwhelming, that there was no longer in it a place for anything small or petty.

They were as gods, no longer just a man and woman but blessed and encompassed by all that was Divine.

"I love you! I adore you and I worship you!" she heard the Prince say. "You are mine, Ancella, mine as you have always been! This, my beloved sweetheart, is where we start living fully, you and I, because now we are complete."

There was a note of triumph in his voice, a kind of exaltation, that made her feel as if it was a clarion call which she could not resist.

She looked up at him and thought that he was like a Crusader starting out to fight for all that was fine and spiritual, and yet at the same time his need for her was very human.

"I love . . . you!" she whispered. "And I . . . believe in you!"

"That is what I wanted to hear, my little darling," he answered. "We must always have faith in each other and faith in our destiny."

Ancella felt desperately ashamed that she had ever doubted him.

"For . . give me," she whispered and knew he understood.

"There is nothing to forgive," he answered. "It was you, my lovely one, who inspired me. You who aroused those aspirations in my mind which could not be crystallised until I met you. Now everything is different. Now, my sweet, we know that because we are together we can reach the top of the world and storm Heaven itself, if necessary!"

As he spoke Ancella felt as if he lifted her again up into the sky. Then his lips were on hers, compelling, demanding, conquering.

She was his completely and absolutely and with a 'conviction' that was unmistakable she knew that whatever the difficulties ahead, their love was eternal.

Other Books by Barbara Cartland

Romantic Novels, over 100, the most recently published being:

The Tears of Love   An Arrow to the Heart
The Devil in Love   The Elusive Earl
Love is Innocent

Autobiographical and Biographical

The Isthmus Years 1919-1939
The Years of Opportunity 1939-1945
I Search for Rainbows 1945-1966
We Danced All Night 1919-1929
Ronald Cartland (with a foreword by Sir Winston Churchill)
Polly, My Wonderful Mother

Historical

Bewitching Women
The Outrageous Queen
(The Story of Queen Christina of Sweden)
The Scandalous Life of King Carol
The Private Life of King Charles II
The Private Life of Elizabeth, Empress of Russia
Josephine, Empress of France
Diane de Poitiers
Metternich – the Passionate Diplomat

Sociology

You in the Home   Etiquette
The Fascinating Forties   The Many Facets of Love
Marriage for Moderns   Sex and the Teenager
Be Vivid, Be Vital   The Book of Charm
Love, Life and Sex   Living Together
Vitamins for Vitality   The Youth Secret
Husbands and Wives

The Magic of Honey

Barbara Cartland's Book of Beauty and Health

Men are Wonderful

Cookery

Barbara Cartland's Health Food Cookery Book
Magic of Honey Cookery Book
Food for Love

Editor of

The Common Problems by Ronald Cartland
(with a preface by the Rt. Hon. The Earl of Selbourne, P.C.)

Drama

Blood Money
French Dressing

Philosophy

Touch the Stars

Radio Operetta

The Rose and the Violet (Music by Mark Lubbock).
Performed in 1942

Radio Plays

The Caged Bird: An episode in the Life of Elizabeth,
Empress of Austria. Performed in 1957

Verse

Lines on Life and Love

Juliette Benzoni

'Juliette Benzoni is a wow of a storyteller'
BOOKS AND BOOKMEN

One Love Is Enough 70p

Introducing Catherine Legoix, a gorgeous new heroine much in the
mould of Angélique, but living and loving in the turbulent Paris
of the fifteenth century.

Violet-eyed Catherine knew only too well the violence, terror and
sensuality of the Hundred Years' War . . . a virgin wife, unwilling
mistress and in love with a man she could not hold.

Catherine and A Time for Love 50p

Cured of leprosy but a prisoner of the Moors – is this to be the
fate of Arnaud, once proud Lord of Montsalvy?

To rescue her husband, Catherine braves the perilous journey from
medieval France to Saracen Spain. Always in danger, she survives
hardship and cruelty, high adventure and razor-edged escapes, to
reach the well-guarded walls of Granada.

Also available:

Catherine 70p
Belle Catherine 70p
Catherine and Arnaud 70p

Georgette Heyer
Sprig Muslin 70p

' "Amanda Smith, I regret to be obliged to inform you that you are a shockingly untruthful girl," said Sir Gareth calmly.'

Amanda looked far too young and too pretty in her gown of sprig muslin to be going about the Regency countryside unattended – it clearly behoved any man of honour, such as that noted Corinthian Sir Gareth Ludlow, to restore her to her family.

Unfortunately, Amanda's determination and lively imagination made this task fraught with difficulty, and involved some of the nicest people in quite reprehensible situations . . .

'The author manages her period conversations with skill and consistency, and her book, at its various levels, is exciting and entertaining. Altogether, it is probably the best thing Miss Heyer has yet done in this kind' PUNCH

Regency Buck 60p

Rich and lovely, ardent and wilful, any restraint maddened Judith Taverner. But in her handsome guardian she met her match – and more.

Julian St John Audley, Fifth Earl of Worth, was one of the Bow-window set, a gamester and excellent whip and a friend of Beau Brummell. Merely thinking of him was enough to put Judith into a rage. Before long she discovered there were other people who also hated her legal guardian . . .

'From the fashionable world of London to the fashionable world of Brighton, Miss Heyer draws the background with an attention to accuracy which is admirable'
THE TIMES LITERARY SUPPLEMENT

Selected bestsellers

- **Jaws** Peter Benchley 70p
- **Let Sleeping Vets Lie** James Herriot 60p
- **If Only They Could Talk** James Herriot 60p
- **It Shouldn't Happen to a Vet** James Herriot 60p
- **Vet in Harness** James Herriot 60p
- **Tinker Tailor Soldier Spy** John le Carré 60p
- **Alive: The Story of the Andes Survivors** (illus)
  Piers Paul Read 75p
- **Gone with the Wind** Margaret Mitchell £1.50
- **Mandingo** Kyle Onstott 75p
- **Shout at the Devil** Wilbur Smith 70p
- **Cashelmara** Susan Howatch £1.25
- **Hotel** Arthur Hailey 80p
- **The Tower** Richard Martin Stern 70p
  (filmed as *The Towering Inferno*)
- **Bonecrack** Dick Francis 60p
- **Jonathan Livingston Seagull** Richard Bach 80p
- **The Fifth Estate** Robin Moore 75p
- **Royal Flash** George MacDonald Fraser 60p
- **The Nonesuch** Georgette Heyer 60p
- **Murder Most Royal** Jean Plaidy 80p
- **The Grapes of Wrath** John Steinbeck 95p

All these books are available at your bookshop or newsagent;
or can be obtained direct from the publisher
Just tick the titles you want and fill in the form below
Prices quoted are applicable in UK

Pan Books, Cavaye Place, London SW10 9PG
Send purchase price plus 15p for the first book and 5p for each
additional book, to allow for postage and packing

Name (block letters)_____

Address_____

_____

While every effort is made to keep prices low, it is sometimes
necessary to increase prices at short notice. Pan Books reserve the
right to show on covers new retail prices which may differ from
those advertised in the text or elsewhere